Alfred Hitchcock's
HAUNTED HOUSEFUL

Alfred
Hitchcock's
HAUNTED
HOUSEFUL

Illustrated by Fred Banbery

RANDOM HOUSE · NEW YORK

The editor gratefully acknowledges the invaluable assistance of Muriel Fuller in the preparation of this volume and thanks the following for permission to include copyrighted material: Manly Wade Wellman and *Boys' Life,* published by the Boy Scouts of America, for "Let's Haunt A House"; Constance Savery for "The Wastwych Secret"; Brandt & Brandt for "Jimmy Takes Vanishing Lessons," Copyright, 1950, by Walter R. Brooks, first published in *Story Parade;* Decie Merwin for "The Mystery of Rabbit Run," by Jack Bechdolt, Copyright, 1946, 1947, by Story Parade, Inc.; Elizabeth Coatsworth for "The Forgotten Island," Copyright, 1942, by Story Parade, Inc.; the Trustees of the Estate of Sir Arthur Conan Doyle and John Murray (Publishers) Ltd. for "The Red Headed League," by Sir Arthur Conan Doyle; Donald Culross Peattie, Louise Redfield Peattie and James Brown Associates, Inc. for "The Mystery in Four-and-a-half Street," Copyright, 1931, 1959, by Donald Culross Peattie and Louise Redfield Peattie.

Introduction

Good evening, ladies and gentlemen, and welcome to my haunted houseful. Visitors are always welcome.

This book is an effort to provide reading for young people who are at the awkward age. Children who are too lazy to walk but still too young to drive. Here are nine stories carefully compiled to furnish reading material in Life's great waiting room where we while away the hours until our driver's license is issued.

I suppose you are wondering why, when the fashion is to put an "Adults Only" sign on books and movies, I am editing a book for younger people. The answer is quite simple. I have previously edited two books of mystery and suspense stories for the older set and the poor dears were frightened silly. In fact, one senior citizen reportedly went completely ape. I do not pretend to know what that absurd expression means but I get the idea and I don't intend to waste a volume of perfectly exquisite ghost stories on people such as that. They just don't have the stomach for it. (Obviously I do.) Of course there may be a few adult delinquents who hold up under experiences with the supernatural, but, let's face it: most of your elders are just plain chicken.

It may seem contradictory, but another reason I am not addressing this book to adults is (and, believe me, this hurts) *they insist they don't believe in ghosts.* It's shocking, really. After all, these are the people who write our country's laws and pay our allowances.

I don't know how they could become so confused. Perhaps you are partly to blame. You have not watched them closely enough and they have fallen in with bad company.

But, as the television repairman often says, the picture is not as black as it seems. There are still many parents who secretly believe. You have probably seen them going through strange rituals and observing peculiar taboos. This morning before breakfast, did you

iii

notice your father lean over and touch his toes repeatedly for no apparent reason? Does your mother go through intermittent periods of fasting? Does she refuse to eat certain, wonderfully rich desserts? Do not be upset. Your parents don't want to talk about it, but some ghost or evil spirit has appeared to them, possibly in their own dressing room, and they are desperately trying to exorcise him.

Why am I publishing a book when I can haunt millions of houses simultaneously each Tuesday night? Certain types of stories make perfect television fare. In the realm of the ghost story, however, I think the printed page has some advantages and I want you to discover them. When you read, you can be alone. —Absolutely alone. Television gives you the comfortable illusion of associating with all those actors. Worst of all, it bathes the entire room in light. Under such circumstances it is amazing that the commercials can be as frightening as they are.

But I have chatted long enough. It is time to get down to business. First, find a room where you can be alone. Comfortable? Uh-uh! Take that transistor radio out of your ear. We want absolute quiet.

Next, turn the light down low. I know; plenty of light is better for your eyes. However, it is death to ghosts and we should always think of others. Now, concentrate on the printed page. . . .

—What's that? You hear a strange noise? I'm sure it's just a shutter banging in the wind. —You don't have shutters? Good! Your attitude indicates you have completed your reading readiness and are all set. You may begin wandering through our little tract of haunted houses. —No, I'm not coming with you. This is as far as I go.

—ALFRED HITCHCOCK

Contents

LET'S HAUNT A HOUSE

MANLY WADE WELLMAN

The wooded slope on which a dozen Scouts of Troop 15 had pitched their week's camp was naturally cheerful. Sun and sky were bright, and the shade was enough. A spring gurgled; there was firewood at hand. But every camper gazed glumly as Assistant Scoutmaster Brimmer drove off in Junior Scoutmaster Sheehan's car to get police help.

On the night before, Mr. Brimmer's car had vanished—without explanation or trace. Not even the lightest sleeper had heard an engine start. Nobody could expect wheel tracks on the rocky downslope from camp, but the soft dirt road below would have shown zigzags to match the distinctive tread of Mr. Brimmer's new tires, and there was nothing but marks of smooth, worn tires. Holmes (Sherlock) Hamilton, leader of the Hound Patrol, knit his black brows to denote a sense of duty shirked.

Sherlock's nickname, his detective hobby, and the fact that his father was Hillwood's police chief should have been enough. If they weren't, Sherlock had one solved mystery to his credit. Dolefully he addressed Assistant Patrol Leader Doc Watson. "No clues, no noises, no tracks. Ghosts must have gobbled it up."

"Maybe ghosts did," volunteered Chuck Schaefer. "The farmers around here say there's a haunted house two miles down the road."

"Leave it to Mr. Palmer," said Doc Watson. He was plump but not soft, and spectacles did not hide his bright eyes. "He's a police sergeant when he's not our Scoutmaster. Mr. Brimmer will bring him back by tonight . . ."

"And Mr. Palmer will explode all the ghost theories." A new voice broke in. Lean, humorous Max Hinkel strolled over from the pit where he had buried some breakfast garbage. "Ghost stories— you sound Middle-Agey, Sherlock."

"I'm not middle-aged," Sherlock punned. "I was fifteen last birthday, and ditto Doc. I don't believe in ghosts, anyway."

"I don't either," chimed in Doc. "I'm just kind of afraid of them."

"Not me," sniffed Max. "Let's visit this haunted house."

The Junior Scoutmaster had planned a morning's hike, and willingly altered the route to follow the road. The Scouts found a waterworn trail branching off, and explored its rocky length until their leader held up his hand for a halt.

"No further," he decreed. "I don't want any nightmares among you boys tonight."

"I see the house down there," said Max, peering into a hollow full of tall, gloomy trees.

It was a lofty old structure, two stories high, with boarded-up windows and an ancient slate roof. Its paint had weathered and faded to a sorrowful gray. Sherlock, too, gazed, then turned to join the departing hikers.

"If there were ghosts, they'd live there in regiments," he said.

"I wouldn't go there after dark," commented Chuck Schaefer, "not for a Congressional Medal."

"Medals are for heroes," scoffed Max. "I'd go there for nothing, just to prove whatever it would prove."

The hike finished and the noon meal eaten, Sherlock brought up the subject again. "You'd visit that haunted house after dark, would you, Max?"

"I read you like a book, Sherlock," replied Max. "You're daring me to visit Creep Castle after sundown."

"Medals are for heroes," Sherlock quoted Max's own words. "Listen to this, Doc. If Max will go there, I'll give him an item for his collection of junk—that Mexican War medal I found."

"It's a deal," said Max. He walked away toward the spring. Doc and Sherlock exchanged grins and winks.

"You know my methods, Watson," said Sherlock softly. "I was going to give him the medal anyway. Now . . ."

"A healthy scare might stir his blood and make him grow?" Doc's habitual grin grew broader. "Count me in."

Sundown brought gloom to the camp site, deeper gloom to the road below. At the point where the trail to the haunted house branched off was the deepest gloom of all.

"Here's where I leave you," Sherlock told Max. He turned off his flashlight, and made his voice sound hollow.

"You'll wait here?" demanded Max, a little defiant, to mask the uneasiness he could not wholly shake off.

"I promised nothing. Get going."

Max moved cautiously over the rough stones. Alone, Sherlock threw off his Scout shirt, displaying a lightweight black jersey. From a pocket he produced a burnt cork and liberally coated his face. He hoped that Doc Watson's stealthy thirty-second start had been time enough for him to reach and enter the house. Doc would wear a sheet to present Max with a white ghost in front; Sherlock would follow behind as a black one. He hurried his preparations to a finish and moved after Max, silent on his canvas sneakers. Separately the two approached the house among the shadowy trees, the unsuspecting Max and the furtive Sherlock.

Mounting the tumble-down porch, Max tugged at the front door. It opened, squeaking and grating like something in a radio horror program. Max peered, then went in. A moment later, Sherlock stole noiselessly after him, sliding along the wall inside.

The front room was musty and still. Max moved over boards that creaked. He stared at a point where one carelessly boarded window gave trifling light, next to some stairs. On the stairs stirred and rustled something pallid and shapeless.

"Ahhhhh," murmured the white thing, and waved draped arms.

Max jumped back, but only two feet. He cleared his throat.

"Come out of that sheet, Doc Watson," he challenged, not very shakily. "Don't you think I know your pudgy outline, even in this light?"

"Ahhhhh," moaned the thing again, and descended a step. Max's eyes, braced wide open, were getting a trifle used to the gloom.

"I know you and your bedding too. I suppose that's your pal Sherlock on the stairs behind you."

"I'm right here," said Sherlock hollowly at Max's shoulder blades.

Max jumped as if somebody had stuck him with a pin.

"Then what's on the stairs with Doc?"

Something towering and black behind the sheeted figure emitted a menacing growl. Max whirled and sprinted out of the door, off the porch, and across the hollow. Behind him, speedy for all his plumpness, hustled Doc Watson, his sheet flapping behind him like a banner. Neither stopped until they had run the length of the rocky terrain and gained the road.

As his feet struck the soft earth, Max stopped so quickly that Doc bumped into him from behind. "Wh-what's that?" quavered Max, pointing unsteadily at something that flapped.

"A shirt on a bush," said Doc. "Sherlock hung it there."

"Where's Sherlock?" demanded Max, staring along the way he had come. "I heard him inside the house."

But neither of them heard him now.

Sherlock still stood against the wall of the old front room, not five feet from the door. The abrupt flight of Max, with Doc at his heels, had delayed Sherlock's own retreat; and the doorway was now blocked by the huge dark shape that had followed Doc downstairs. It stood long and motionlessly, uttering no sound beyond heavy breathing. Then it turned heavily and faced the interior, lingering on the threshold. Sherlock held his own breath, glad of the dark jersey and the burnt cork that he had donned to frighten Max. Now they helped him blend into the darkness.

"Well?" came a harsh, high voice from upstairs, making Sherlock's curls crawl with shocked terror. "What was it?"

The big thing in the doorway made a gruff sound in its throat, and replied in a voice as deep as a bullfrog's. "Can't be sure, Corey. You were in the attic, huh? I was just opening a can of hash in the upstairs back room when I heard feet down here, on the stairs. I started down as quiet as I could, and somebody else came in. They talked together—sounded like kids. Then one of 'em saw me and they went out of here like dogs with cans tied to 'em."

"Did you see 'em plain outside?" demanded the high voice.

"For just a second. They dusted away under the trees faster'n my eyes could follow, let alone me. They sounded like kids . . ."

"But maybe they weren't, Corey," finished the high voice.

The footsteps that came downstairs sounded light and active, like a small, spry man. "You were smart not to go after 'em. Somebody might have had a gun."

"Strike a light," said the big fellow called Corey, and Sherlock felt his tongue grow dry between his teeth. But the other man made an ugly noise of scornful refusal.

"Won't you ever learn, Corey? Anybody watching could see the light between the boards on the windows. We stay dark in here after sundown, like I told you when we first came. The hicks around here give the place plenty of leeway, with all the ghost stories about it; but lights might bring dicks instead of hicks."

Corey came back inside and pulled the door shut. He turned—

Sherlock thought Corey was coming his way, and retreated along the wall as silently as he could. But there was a creak as a heavy weight settled on an old chair. "Come on down, Stubs," Corey urged his companion. "Let's listen for a while before we turn in."

Stubs descended the stairs and sat on the bottom step. Sherlock saw him dimly in the feeble light that hung there. He was as short as his name, but built for action, with wide shoulders and narrow hips and a head carried alertly upright. Something clinked—Stubs had laid a metal object on the step beside him. A gun?

"It's gonta be lonesome here," complained Corey. "Three days and nights in this spook hole, and I feel spooky myself."

"Good," Stubs rejoined. "The local yokels expect spooks. Maybe what we're doing has its drawbacks, but it's better than working, isn't it?"

"And you can't beat the hours," said Corey, his good humor a little restored. "We ain't done bad so far. We got one night before last, another last night, and you say you spotted another we can get tomorrow night. Pull 'em to pieces, and eighty-eight garages hungry for parts will push and scramble to pay our prices . . ."

Sherlock had continued to move along the wall, silent on sneaker-clad feet, as he had learned to do in many a night game. He hugged the wall, so that floor boards would not creak. A gust of cool air fanned his cork-smeared cheek, and he put out a hand and found the edge of an open door. Corey and Stubs chattered on and he crouched down to back through the doorway into the next room.

For an instant of horror he feared there was no next room. His backward-groping foot could not find a floor to stand on, and only a quick, noiseless grab for the door-jamb kept him from falling. Then his foot stretched lower and touched solid wood. Another stairway here, going down—Sherlock painfully descended another step, another. He groped around a turn in the stairs and to a door below tightly closed.

For long minutes he waited, hand on latch, until Stubs said

something in his harsh high voice that set both men laughing in the room above. Under cover of the whoops, Sherlock lifted the latch, slipped through, and closed the door behind him.

It was darker here than upstairs. He knelt and touched a cement floor, then a cement wall. Sniffing, he detected an oily smell. Upstairs Corey and Stubs discussed something, but he could not make out the words. From his pocket he drew his flashlight, paused to gather all his powers of attention. Then he flashed it on, held it for two seconds, and flashed it off again.

He had seen a big rectangular chamber, with double doors at the far end. These must lead to an entry from lower ground behind the house. The basement itself was furnished with a long bench of dark wood along one wall, with boxes upon it, and larger crates and kegs underneath it. Nearer the double doors was a jumble of big, irregular shapes, covered with old blankets and tarpaulins. Sherlock tiptoed gingerly toward where he had seen the bench.

He pawed for and found its corner. Next he groped into a box, and lifted out something that felt like an ornamental cap for the radiator of an automobile. Returning it, he felt other things in the box—spark plugs, he decided. Another box held more small parts for an automobile—no, much more than enough for one car.

What had Stubs said? A job that's better than working. The men had mentioned garages. Was this a garage? Why run a garage here, and why hide it if they were running it?

Feeling his way along the bench, he touched something with his toe and stooped to investigate. A cylinder head, he guessed, and beside it three more. Beyond he came upon axle rods leaning against the wall beyond the bench, and, afraid of knocking them down, he gave them wide berth and continued on to the double doors.

But he found that they were padlocked shut, and turned back to the bulks swathed in blankets and tarpaulins. Perhaps he could hide among them until morning, then find his way upstairs and out.

The nearest tarpaulin covered a heap of fenders. No dents or breaks—they were certainly not here for repair. Next he uncovered a stack of tires, still on their rims. He prodded the uppermost. Tires; he remembered the mystery of the morning. His fingers quested along the tread of one, then another.

The pattern was sharp-cut, new, and recognizable. He and the other Scouts had searched for its marks short hours ago. The rear tires of Mr. Brimmer's vanished car had been patterned in just that zigzag fashion.

"Now I know!"

He opened his mouth to say it aloud, and stopped just in time. He almost knew, really, but very shortly he would make sure. He lifted off the two zigzag-treaded tires, then two more that must have shod Mr. Brimmer's front wheels. The tires below were worn smooth, like the tires that had made the marks in the road, marks disregarded by himself and others. He lifted one, and found it strangely heavy. It still contained the complete wheel.

"I do know!"

And when the knowledge drove into his mind, perhaps he could be excused for dropping the wheel, and knocking over the whole stack of tires with a heavy echoing thump.

Instantly the voices upstairs fell silent. He heard Stubs and Corey get to their feet. He heard the floor creak as they moved cautiously but purposefully toward the basement stairs, the heavy feet of Corey and the surer, lighter feet of Stubs.

Caught, Sherlock told himself wretchedly. There were only two ways out of the basement—one padlocked, the other being descended by the men who were after him. He must think of something brilliant and decisive, something that would give him the right to the nickname of Sherlock, or inside of brief seconds . . .

Sherlock! Of course, it was in Sherlock Holmes! Not in the stories, but in the play. He himself had never seen William Gillette as the great detective, but his father had often told him about it. The big scene especially lived in his imagination. A dark room, murderous villains, and how Sherlock Holmes had misdirected their attack.

He snapped on his flashlight, ran to the bench, and set it there so that its beam made a halo of radiance at the door. Light must have seeped at once through the cracks, for the men, halfway downstairs, paused.

"Guns, Corey," Sherlock heard Stubs say. His heart racing and his lip caught in his teeth, Sherlock tiptoed to the door and stood next to its hinges. A hand rattled the latch, lifted it. The door was thrown open, screening him from the rest of the cellar.

"There he is!" Stubs yelled furiously. "Slap him full of lead!"

Revolver shots rang in the cellar like a bombardment. Both Stubs and Corey were snarling and shouting as they charged the light after their volley. As they cleared the door Sherlock spun into it and darted up the stairs. He tripped on the top one, but kept his feet. Four mighty leaps carried him to the front door. He wrenched it open and ran as Max and Doc had done, making for the trail that led to the road.

Racing along the stony path, he strained his eyes to see ahead. Almost at the road, he came to a halt. A car was parked squarely across the head of the trail, and figures moved stealthily toward him. Allies of Corey and Stubs? He tried to turn and flee back the way he had come, but bumped into a tree, and cried out despite himself.

"That you, Sherlock?" called Doc Watson.

"Take it easy," said someone else. It was Sergeant Palmer, his Scoutmaster, pushing close with a grim expression on his normally pleasant face. Others gathered around Sherlock—Max, Doc, Mr. Brimmer, and a broad-bodied stranger who wore the star that identified the township constable.

"We made it to camp in about eight jumps," Doc told Sherlock pantingly. "Mr. Brimmer was back with Sergeant Palmer, and he and the constable drove down here to find out . . ."

"It's all solved," Sherlock cut in hurriedly. "I've been down in the cellar of the place. There are two men stealing cars. I found parts of Mr. Brimmer's car, and of two or three others. They're stripping the stolen cars for parts, tires and so on, and are selling them secondhand."

"That's why," said Mr. Brimmer. "But how did they get my car away without our hearing it or finding the tire marks?"

"I found that out, too," said Sherlock. "Stacked with your tires were other smooth-worn old tires, with your wheels still inside them. That explains it. They sneaked up and switched the tires so we couldn't see any tread patterns we knew. And they could roll the car downhill without starting the motor."

Sergeant Palmer was moving along the trail again. "Careful," Sherlock called softly. "They have guns. They shot at me—that is, they shot at where I made them think I was."

"You've given us enough information, Sherlock," Sergeant Palmer told him. "Keep quiet. You and the others stay at the rear. Constable, you and I will go up the trail at either side"

He slid in among the trees to the right, the constable to the left, and both stole in the direction of the house. They had not gone a score of paces before the sound of feet—a pair of heavy feet, another pair of light ones—came toward them from the hollow.

Sergeant Palmer paused behind a trunk that would turn any bullet, and drew his police revolver. His other hand flashed a light along the trail, and in its glow two figures stopped and made as if to run.

"You're under arrest," snapped the sergeant quickly. "Drop those guns and hold up your hands."

There were two clinks on the stones, and the men glumly lifted their arms.

"Okay, you win," squealed Stubs angrily. "You got us surrounded."

The constable and Sergeant Palmer closed in, quickly snatching up the two fallen revolvers. The others came up to watch. Sherlock had a good look at his enemies for the first time.

"Surrounded?" Palmer took time to repeat.

"Sure. Back at the house—how'd your pal slip into the basement? We shot his flashlight full of holes, but we didn't get him. If he's coming up behind us, yell out that we've quit. I don't want no slugs in my back."

The constable had brought out a pair of handcuffs, and now he shackled Corey's right wrist to Stub's left. Sergeant Palmer slid his revolver back into its holster and chuckled.

"I only know half the story so far," he told the prisoners, "but we didn't have anybody there—no other peace officers, at least. This boy"—and he clapped Sherlock on the shoulder—"was the one who found out what you were up to, and scared you into thinking you were surrounded."

Corey and Stubs glared at Sherlock. Corey moistened his lips. "Good night! Boy Scouts," he grumbled. "What's your name, kid?"

"Just call him Sherlock," piped up Doc Watson.

THE WASTWYCH SECRET

CONSTANCE SAVERY

When we were children we lived with Grandmamma and Grandpapa Wastwych in their house on the borders of the gray-green marshes. Our parents were in Africa; and we had lived at Marigolds for so long that we had lost all memory of our former life, and Mamma and Papa were only pleasant dreamland names.

We were happy children, living quiet sunny lives without shadow or event. If we were a little afraid of stern Grandpapa Wastwych, in his white ruffled shirts and brown velvet clothes and gold repeater, we ardently admired our gay and gracious grandmamma with the blue eyes and silvery hair. To our childish minds, she seemed the soul of goodness and dignity and charm; in all the

13

countryside there was no old lady who could compare with her. To rebel against Grandmamma's decisions, to question her wishes, to doubt her wisdom and righteousness—these were crimes beyond the range of our wildest thoughts.

So, on the day when Jessica Fairlie came to drink tea with us, we naturally spoke much of Grandmamma in our efforts to entertain our guest. Jessica was neat and ladylike, with small features and pale gold ringlets. We feared her at first sight; and before tea was over, we knew that she was indeed a person to be respected. She attended a school for young ladies; she was fond of needlework; she thought most games rough and all boys objectionable; she was trusted to pay long visits to her relations all by herself, without a nurse. In fact, our possession of a wonderfully clever and interesting grandmamma was the only point in our favor; in all else we were hopelessly inferior to our visitor.

After tea, therefore, we tried to show her how marvelous a grandmamma we had. We escorted her to a corner of the drawing room and showed her Grandmamma's first sampler.

"Look," we said. "Grandmamma did that when she was six."

We were justly proud of the sampler, for in each corner stood a red flowerpot containing a small orange tree with green leaves and golden fruit. In the middle were the words:

> *Worked by me, Jane Caroline,*
> *In the year eighteen hundred and nine.*

Grandmamma had composed the poetry herself, which shows how very clever she was, even at six years old.

Jessica blinked her pale eyes and said that the sampler was beautiful. Then we took her to see a model under a glass shade— a basket filled with pears and plums and grapes made in wax. Jessica admired it very much and would hardly believe that Grandmamma had really made it.

Next we took her to show her Grandmamma's dried herbs and her pickles and ointments and spices and preserves; and we begged Margery, the still-room maid, to give us a little parsley jelly in a saucer for Jessica, who had never tasted it. Grandmamma's parsley jelly had a surprising and disagreeable taste, but the color was charming—it was a delicate pale green. Jessica shuddered at the first mouthful and put down the spoon in haste.

After that we showed her some white skeleton leaves and our doll's feather furniture, all of which Grandmamma's clever fingers had made for us. Jessica's eyes became as round as sea pebbles. She said, "I would like to see your grandmamma."

We took her to the window, for we had heard Grandmamma's voice in the drive below. There stood Grandmamma, broom in hand, helping the garden boy to clear away the leaves. She was wearing a great dark blue cloak with a peaked hood; and in spite of her odd attire she looked as dignified as possible.

Jessica studied her hard for a full minute. Then she said, "I'm going home now."

"Why, you have not played with us yet," we protested.

"I am going home now," replied Jessica.

And she went. The next day we met her taking a walk with her aunt's maid. Nurse Grimmitt and the maid were friendly, so Jessica was told to walk on ahead with Nonie, Tawny and me.

"Why did you go home so early yesterday?" asked Tawny.

Jessica looked round to make sure that Nurse Grimmitt and the maid could not hear.

"I will tell you if you like," she said mysteriously. "It was because of your grandmamma."

"Because of Grandmamma?" we echoed in confusion and amazement.

"Yes," said Jessica, speaking very calmly. "Your grandmamma is a witch, and I do not like witches."

I cannot well describe the effect her words had upon us; but I know that the sun began to jump here and there in the sky and that cold shuddering thrills ran through our little bodies.

"Grandmamma is not a witch!" gasped Nonie.

"Oh yes, she is," Jessica assured us. "I am quite sure of it. When I heard her name, I thought that it was a witch's name; for of course a witch would be called 'Was-a-witch.'"

"It's 'Wastwych,'" we remonstrated timidly.

"Then that is even worse," returned Jessica, "because 'Wastwich' must mean 'Was-the-witch,' as if she were a particularly dreadful one who was more important than the rest. And I have other proofs. First of all, there is that sampler. No one who was not a witch could possibly have done such a clever piece of work as that. Then there was her horrible jelly, which was just the kind of thing a witch would make. And you yourselves said that she made preserves from sloes and elderberries and crabapples—and of course they are all witchy jams, every one of them. And then nobody but a witch could make leaves turn into skeletons and feathers into dolls' furniture."

"Nonsense!" said Tawny.

Jessica looked at him coldly.

"Listen to me, little boy," she said. "I know all about witches, because there used to be one in our village, and because my papa has a large book on witchcraft in his study. I should not say that your grandmamma was a witch unless I had very good reasons for saying it. Here is another reason—your grandmamma dresses like a witch. I have never seen an ordinary old lady in a blue cloak with a peaked hood!"

We were dumb. Jessica went on impressively, "I have still one more proof; and when you have heard it, I think you will be obliged to confess that what I say is true. Your grandmamma rides over the marshes on her broomstick to visit the Will-o'-the-Wisp."

"She doesn't!" we cried, midway between terror and belief.

"There is a Will-o'-the-Wisp on the marshes—you can't deny it," replied Jessica with finality.

"Grandpapa says that it is only the light from a little hut where poachers sometimes lurk," said Nonie.

"Aunt's maid says it is a Will-o'-the-Wisp," Jessica said firmly. "We can see it from our house. And every evening just after six o'clock an old woman in a blue cloak goes gliding along the marshes to that light. The first time I saw her she was carrying a broom! I see her every night while I am being put to bed. It is your grandmamma. She walks very fast in spite of the pools and quagmires, and on dark nights she carries a horn lantern. She comes home at seven o'clock, gliding over the ground. If you don't believe me, just you watch what she does between six and seven to-night."

We looked at one another in dismay; for strangely enough Grandmamma had lately developed a curious habit of vanishing from the house just at that time. Jessica saw her advantage.

"It is a great disgrace to have a witch in one's family," she said. "Of course, she may be a harmless white witch, but there is never any knowing. I wonder what your friends would think if they could know that your grandmamma was a witch. I am afraid that they would never speak to you again, or to her, either."

"Oh, don't tell any one, Jessica!" we implored.

"I do not know whether it would be right to keep such a dreadful secret," said Jessica. "Suppose she cast a spell over my Aunt Matilda, or blighted the gooseberry bushes in the garden?"

In a moment of time Nonie and I saw ourselves outcasts, witch-children to whom nobody would speak.

"Oh, Jessica, don't tell!" I pleaded. "Here is my little mother-of-pearl penknife—you may have it if you care to take it."

"And here is my mole and blue satin bag," said Nonie, hurriedly thrusting it into Jessica's willing hand. "Dear Jessica, you will not tell?"

"I will think it over," said Jessica. "I will keep the matter a secret for at least one day."

Then the maid summoned her; and we went home with Nurse Grimmitt, our steps dragging as if our shoes were weighted with lead. It seemed unutterably wicked to suspect our dear, beautiful grandmamma of witchcraft; and yet Jessica had produced such an appalling array of proofs that our hearts sank when we remembered them. Our only comfort was in Tawny, who stoutly declared that he did not believe a word of Jessica's crazy talk. His courage went far to revive our flagging spirits; and when we saw Grandmamma sewing peacefully in the drawing room at home, we actually ventured to laugh at Jessica's story.

Nevertheless, Nonie and I felt restless and uneasy when the hour of six drew nigh.

"Estelle," said Nonie, "do you think it would be very wrong for us to slip into the garden to see where Grannie walks at night? For if she does not go over the marshes, we may feel quite, quite certain that she is not a—you know what. I shall not believe any of those other proofs if only we can be sure that Jessica was mistaken about the marshes."

"Perhaps it is best to make sure," I agreed, though my heart beat

fast at the thought of such an adventure. I wished that Tawny could have come with us, but he always spent the hour between six and seven over a Latin lesson with our austere grandpapa. We must fare forth unaided and alone.

Soon we were waiting in the dark shadow of some bushes close by a gate that opened on the marshes, lying all silvery green in the moonlight, with dusky patches of water here and there ringed with treacherous sucking moss. Very cruel and dangerous were the marshes, smile as they might beneath their summer carpet of king-cups and cuckoo-flowers, and peaceful as they looked under winter moon and stars. Far off we could see the dim blue glimmer from Will-o'-the-Wisp's house; and we shivered as we lingered in the cold, waiting to see what would happen.

Then a door opened softly, stealthily, and a tall figure in a peaked blue hood came down the path. We needed not to be told whose figure it was; for no one save Grandmamma walked with that firm, swift tread. In fear-filled silence we watched her open the gate and step out on to the marshes, walking with such sure, rapid steps that she seemed almost to fly over the ground. Nonie and I needed no further proof. We clasped each other's hands and went back in misery to the house.

I am glad to remember that never for an instant did we fear any personal harm from Grandmamma's witcheries. We were too fond of her to dream that she might hurt us—all that we dreaded was the disgrace that would fall on a family known to have a witch in it. Of that shame and horror we could not bear to think.

Apart from Tawny's sturdy faith in Grandmamma, we had nothing to comfort us in our distress. We dared not confide in Nurse, and Jessica was most unkind. When we next met her, she questioned us strictly; and after she had made us own that we had seen Grandmamma on the marshes, she nodded her head in satisfaction.

"But you won't tell?" we pleaded.

"I think that people ought to know," said Jessica. It was not easy to persuade her to keep our secret a little longer. In the end we gained a week's grace, but in order to obtain it we were obliged to offer her one of our best dolls, a needlecase with a green satin cover, and three cedarwood pencils. As soon as the week was over she met us again, determined to reveal all she knew. Once more we bribed her, this time with my red necklace of coral flowers.

After that, we had to make her a present every day. One by one our dearest treasures disappeared from our three toy-cupboards, for Jessica would never take anything less than the best. In spite of her fear of witches, she became bold enough to invite herself to play with us, so that she might choose her presents more conveniently.

We did not enjoy Jessica's visits. When she came, we sat in silent grief, knowing that our hearts would soon be wrung with sorrow. When she went, we hid in our toy-cupboards, crying. But we never thought of resisting. She had all she wanted.

Little by little the toy-cupboards were emptied until there came a dreadful day when Jessica turned away with the disdainful words, "There is nothing worth taking. You have very few toys."

"We used to have plenty," said Tawny.

"I am going to drink tea with the Miss Forrests tomorrow," said Jessica. "They have a much larger playroom than yours, and your baby house is nothing in comparison with theirs. I have told them that there is a secret about your grandmamma, and they are very curious to hear it."

"But you won't tell, Jessica?" we entreated for the hundredth time. "Think of all the things we have given you—all the gilt tables and chairs from our baby house and Tawny's whip and his ninepins and his Chinese doll and the jumping frog and the book of fairy tales and the tea-set and . . ."

Jessica looked at us with a cold eye.

"I am afraid that I cannot keep such a wicked secret any longer," she answered. "I have always known that it was wrong to keep secrets about witches; but in order to oblige you I have kept your secret for three weeks and three days. And Blanche and Fanny Forrest are anxious to know it.

"They will tell everyone!" we said.

"You should not have a witch for your grandmamma," said Jessica. "I shall not come to your house again, for I do not care to 'sociate with the grandchildren of a witch."

Then she went away. Had the sun fallen out of the sky, we could hardly have been more dismayed. Tawny spoke quickly.

"I do not believe that Grandmamma is a witch," he said. "I have never believed it. I will follow her over the marshes this very evening, and I will watch what happens. And then I shall tell Jessica the truth."

"But we are forbidden to set foot on the marshes!" I protested.

"I know that," said Tawny.

"And Grandpapa will punish you for missing your Latin lesson," said Nonie. "He will be angry, because you'll not be able to tell him why you went to the marshes."

"I know that, too," said Tawny.

"It is dangerous on the marshes," I said feebly. "And—and, Tawny, suppose you find out that Grandmamma really is a . . ."

Tawny gave me a look of great contempt, rose, and walked to the door.

Nonie and I did not venture to follow him. We knelt on the window seat and watched the dark shadows dancing outside. Presently Grandmamma's tall figure passed by, and a little later a small black object crept out of the bushes and followed her.

After a while we heard Grandpapa's voice calling angrily for Tawny. Shaking in our shoes, we hid behind the curtains, but Grandpapa saw us.

We were dreadfully afraid of Grandpapa in a temper. When he made us stand like culprits before him, we could not think how to evade his first angry question as to Tawny's whereabouts. Nonie wept and said, "He has gone to find out whether Grandmamma is a witch."

"You impudent little girl!" roared Grandpapa. "What do you mean?"

He looked so fierce that we could scarcely bring ourselves to reply. Making a vast effort, we said, "Jessica Fairlie said that

Grandmamma was so clever she must be a witch. Jessica said that only witches made parsley jelly and wild-fruit jam and samplers with poetry and furniture out of feathers and wore peaked hoods."

I think that if Grandpapa had been any angrier he would have burst.

"How dare you—how dare you?" he said. "You believed such rubbish as that?"

"Not quite, Grandpapa," we sobbed. "You see, Jessica said that Grandmamma flew over the marshes every night at six o'clock on her broomstick to visit the Will-o'-the-Wisp. And we watched—and Grandmamma did do it. We did not see the broomstick, but we saw Grandmamma. So then we thought that she must be a witch. And Tawny wouldn't believe it, but he has gone to find out why Grandmamma walks over the marshes so that he may tell Jessica that it isn't true."

Grandpapa's purple color faded away.

"Tawny on the marshes at night! He will be sucked under and drowned!"

And forgetting his anger, he dashed down the stairs like a young man and rushed to the marsh gate, with Nonie and me after him. And there at the gate stood Tawny, dripping from head to foot with the cruel black mud of the quagmires. Grandpapa was so glad to see him safe and sound that anger had no time to return.

"Well, sir, I hope you are satisfied that your grandmamma is not a witch," he said.

Tawny saw that Grandpapa knew.

"It is not the Will-o'-the-Wisp that Grandmamma visits," he said. "It is a man who is ill and who lives in the Will's hut all alone. He had blue eyes like Grandmamma. I saw him through the window. Grandmamma gave him broth to drink. And there was a broomstick in the corner, but she did not ride on it. I fell in the pools coming home. Grandmamma is coming now on her feet. She is not a witch at all. May I go to Jessica's house to tell her?"

"You may go to bed!" said Grandpapa. "I will tell Miss Jessica myself." His face wore a most peculiar expression.

Then Grandmamma stepped lightly in at the marsh-gate and gave a cry of alarm at the sight of us all standing there. Grandpapa looked at her horn lantern and basket. "It's that rascal Humphrey, I suppose?"

We did not understand, but Grandmamma did.

"He dared not come home, Richard," she said. "He is ill from want and misery—he sought shelter in the hut and sent word by old Nurse to me. Oh, Richard, forgive him!"

Grandpapa made her a courtly bow.

"Jane, God in His Mercy has preserved us from a great sorrow this night. For that reason, if for no other, I cannot refuse forgiveness to my son. If he is able to come with me, I will go now to bring him home."

Then Grandmamma put her horn lantern into his hand, her face alight with happiness. And Grandpapa walked away over the marshes with slow and ponderous tread.

Jessica never told her secret, for she did not drink tea with the Miss Forrests after all. She went home to her papa and mamma instead and her Aunt Matilda sent our toys back to us in an enormous parcel by the maid. But the secret escaped none the less. We did not tell it, Grandpapa did not, and Uncle Humphrey did not, and Nurse Grimmitt never knew it; so we were at a loss to imagine how it leaked out. We did not think that Grandmamma could have told it; for not even such a very gay grandmamma as ours would have liked people to know that two out of her three grandchildren had actually suspected her of being a witch! Yet everyone knew, and everyone teased us. Once we had the supreme mortification of hearing the Misses Forrest say to their new governess, "Look, there are the silly children who thought that their Grandmamma Wastwych was a witch!"

JIMMY TAKES VANISHING LESSONS

WALTER R. BROOKS

The school bus picked up Jimmy Crandall every morning at the side road that led up to his aunt's house, and every afternoon it dropped him there again. And so twice a day, on the bus, he passed the entrance to the mysterious road.

It wasn't much of a road any more. It was choked with weeds and blackberry bushes, and the woods on both sides pressed in so closely that the branches met overhead, and it was dark and gloomy even on bright days. The bus driver once pointed it out.

"Folks that go in there after dark," he said, "well, they usually don't ever come out again. There's a haunted house about a quarter of a mile down that road." He paused. "But you ought to know about that, Jimmy. It was your grandfather's house."

Jimmy knew about it, and he knew that it now belonged to his Aunt Mary. But Jimmy's aunt would never talk to him about the house. She said the stories about it were silly nonsense and there were no such things as ghosts. If all the villagers weren't a lot of superstitious idiots, she would be able to rent the house, and then she would have enough money to buy Jimmy some decent clothes and take him to the movies.

Jimmy thought it was all very well to say that there were no such things as ghosts, but how about the people who had tried to live there? Aunt Mary had rented the house three times, but every family had moved out within a week. They said the things that went on there were just too queer. So nobody would live in it any more.

Jimmy thought about the house a lot. If he could only prove that there wasn't a ghost . . . And one Saturday when his aunt was in the village, Jimmy took the key to the haunted house from its hook on the kitchen door, and started out.

It had seemed like a fine idea when he had first thought of it— to find out for himself. Even in the silence and damp gloom of the old road it still seemed pretty good. Nothing to be scared of, he told himself. Ghosts aren't around in the daytime. But when he came out in the clearing and looked at those blank, dusty windows, he wasn't so sure.

"Oh, come on!" he told himself. And he squared his shoulders and waded through the long grass to the porch.

Then he stopped again. His feet did not seem to want to go up the steps. It took him nearly five minutes to persuade them to move. But when at last they did, they marched right up and across the porch to the front door, and Jimmy set his teeth hard and put the key in the keyhole. It turned with a squeak. He pushed the door open and went in.

That was probably the bravest thing that Jimmy had ever done. He was in a long dark hall with closed doors on both sides, and on the right there were stairs going up. He had left the door open behind him, and the light from it showed him that, except for the hatrack and table and chairs, the hall was empty. And then as he stood there, listening to the bumping of his heart, gradually the light faded, the hall grew darker and darker—as if something huge had come up on the porch behind him and stood there, blocking the doorway. He swung round quickly, but there was nothing there.

He drew a deep breath. It must have been just a cloud passing across the sun. But then the door, all by itself, began to swing shut. And before he could stop it, it closed with a bang. And it was then, as he was pulling frantically at the handle to get out, that Jimmy saw the ghost.

It behaved just as you would expect a ghost to behave. It was a tall, dim, white figure, and it came gliding slowly down the stairs towards him. Jimmy gave a yell, yanked the door open, and tore down the steps.

He didn't stop until he was well down the road. Then he had to get his breath. He sat down on a log. "Boy!" he said. "I've seen a ghost! Golly, was that awful!" Then after a minute, he thought, "What was so awful about it? He was trying to scare me, like that smart aleck who was always jumping out from behind things. Pretty silly business for a grown-up ghost to be doing."

It always makes you mad when someone deliberately tries to scare you. And as Jimmy got over his fright, he began to get angry. And pretty soon he got up and started back. "I must get that key, anyway," he thought, for he had left it in the door.

This time he approached very quietly. He thought he'd just lock the door and go home. But as he tiptoed up the steps he saw it was still open; and as he reached out cautiously for the key, he heard a faint sound. He drew back and peeked around the door-jamb, and there was the ghost.

The ghost was going back upstairs, but he wasn't gliding now, he was doing a sort of dance, and every other step he would bend double and shake with laughter. His thin cackle was the sound Jimmy had heard. Evidently he was enjoying the joke he had played.

That made Jimmy madder than ever. He stuck his head farther around the doorjamb and yelled "Boo!" at the top of his lungs. The ghost gave a thin shriek and leaped two feet in the air, then collapsed on the stairs.

As soon as Jimmy saw he could scare the ghost even worse than the ghost could scare him, he wasn't afraid any more, and he came right into the hall. The ghost was hanging on the banister and panting. "Oh, my goodness!" he gasped. "Oh, my gracious! Boy, you can't do that to me!"

"I did it, didn't I?" said Jimmy. "Now we're even."

"Nothing of the kind," said the ghost crossly. "You seem pretty stupid, even for a boy. Ghosts are supposed to scare people.

People aren't supposed to scare ghosts." He got up slowly and glided down and sat on the bottom step. "But look here, boy; this could be pretty serious for me if people got to know about it."

"You mean you don't want me to tell anybody about it?" Jimmy asked.

"Suppose we make a deal," the ghost said. "You keep still about this, and in return I'll—well, let's see; how would you like to know how to vanish?"

"Oh, that would be swell!" Jimmy exclaimed. "But—can you vanish?"

"Sure," said the ghost, and he did. All at once he just wasn't there. Jimmy was alone in the hall.

But his voice went right on. "It would be pretty handy, wouldn't it?" he said persuasively. "You could get into the movies free whenever you wanted to, and if your aunt called you to do something—when you were in the yard, say—well, she wouldn't be able to find you."

"I don't mind helping Aunt Mary," Jimmy said.

"H'm. High-minded, eh?" said the ghost. "Well, then . . ."

"I wish you'd please reappear," Jimmy interrupted. "It makes me feel funny to talk to somebody who isn't there"

"Sorry, I forgot," said the ghost, and there he was again, sitting on the bottom step. Jimmy could see the step, dimly, right through him. "Good trick, eh? Well, if you don't like vanishing, maybe I could teach you to seep through keyholes. Like this." He floated over to the door and went right through the keyhole, the way water goes down the drain. Then he came back the same way.

"That's useful, too," he said. "Getting into locked rooms and so on. You can go anywhere the wind can."

"No," said Jimmy. "There's only one thing you can do to get me to promise not to tell about scaring you. Go live somewhere else. There's Miller's up the road. Nobody lives there any more."

"That old shack!" said the ghost, with a nasty laugh. "Doors and windows half off, roof leaky—no thanks! What do you think it's like in a storm, windows banging, rain dripping on you—I guess not! Peace and quiet, that's really what a ghost wants out of life."

"Well, I don't think it's very fair," Jimmy said, "for you to live in a house that doesn't belong to you and keep my aunt from renting it."

"Pooh!" said the ghost. "I'm not stopping her from renting it. I don't take up any room, and it's not my fault if people get scared and leave."

"It certainly is!" Jimmy said angrily. "You don't play fair and I'm not going to make any bargain with you. I'm going to tell everybody how I scared you."

"Oh, you mustn't do that!" The ghost seemed quite disturbed and he vanished and reappeared rapidly several times. "If that got out, every ghost in the country would be in terrible trouble."

So they argued about it. The ghost said if Jimmy wanted money he could learn to vanish; then he could join a circus and get a big salary. Jimmy said he didn't want to be in a circus; he wanted to go to college and learn to be a doctor. He was very firm. And the ghost began to cry. "But this is my home, boy," he said. "Thirty years I've lived here and no trouble to anybody, and now you want to throw me out into the cold world! And for what? A little money! That's pretty heartless." And he sobbed, trying to make Jimmy feel cruel.

Jimmy didn't feel cruel at all, for the ghost had certainly driven plenty of other people out into the cold world. But he didn't really think it would do much good for him to tell anybody that he had scared the ghost. Nobody would believe him, and how could he prove it? So after a minute he said, "Well, all right. You teach me to vanish and I won't tell." They settled it that way.

Jimmy didn't say anything to his aunt about what he'd done. But every Saturday he went to the haunted house for his vanishing lesson. It is really quite easy when you know how, and in a couple of weeks he could flicker, and in six weeks the ghost gave him an examination and he got a B plus, which is very good for a human. So he thanked the ghost and shook hands with him and said, "Well, good-by now. You'll hear from me."

"What do you mean by that?" said the ghost suspiciously. But Jimmy just laughed and ran off home.

That night at supper Jimmy's aunt said, "Well, what have you been doing today?"

"I've been learning to vanish."

His aunt smiled and said, "That must be fun."

"Honestly," said Jimmy. "The ghost up at grandfather's house taught me."

"I don't think that's very funny," said his aunt. "And will you please not—why, where are you?" she demanded, for he had vanished.

"Here, Aunt Mary," he said as he reappeared.

"Merciful heavens!" she exclaimed, and she pushed back her chair and rubbed her eyes hard. Then she looked at him again.

Well, it took a lot of explaining and he had to do it twice more before he could persuade her that he really could vanish. She was pretty upset. But at last she calmed down and they had a long talk. Jimmy kept his word and didn't tell her that he had scared the ghost, but he said he had a plan and at last, though very reluctantly, she agreed to help him.

So the next day she went up to the old house and started to work. She opened the windows and swept and dusted and aired the bedding, and made as much noise as possible. This disturbed the ghost, and pretty soon he came floating into the room where she was sweeping. She was scared all right. She gave a yell and threw the broom at him. As the broom went right through him and he came nearer, waving his arms and groaning, she shrank back.

And Jimmy, who had been standing there invisible all the time, suddenly appeared and jumped at the ghost with a "Boo!" And the ghost fell over in a dead faint.

As soon as Jimmy's aunt saw that, she wasn't frightened any more. She found some smelling salts and held them under the ghost's nose, and when he came to she tried to help him into a chair. Of course, she couldn't help him much because her hands went right through him. But at last he sat up and said reproachfully to Jimmy, "You broke your word!"

"I promised not to tell about scaring you," said the boy, "but I didn't promise not to scare you again."

And his aunt said, "You really are a ghost, aren't you? I thought you were just stories people made up. Well, excuse me, but I must get on with my work." And she began sweeping and banging around with her broom harder than ever.

The ghost put his hands to his head. "All this noise," he said. "Couldn't you work more quietly, ma'am?"

"Whose house is this, anyway?" she demanded. "If you don't like it, why don't you move out?"

The ghost sneezed violently several times. "Excuse me," he said. "You're raising so much dust. Where's that boy?" he asked suddenly. For Jimmy had vanished again.

"I'm sure I don't know," she replied. "Probably getting ready to scare you again."

"You ought to have better control of him," said the ghost severely. "If he was my boy, I'd take a hairbrush to him."

"You have my permission," she said, and she reached right through the ghost and pulled the chair cushion out from under him and began banging the dust out of it. "What's more," she went on, as he got up and glided wearily to another chair, "Jimmy and I are going to sleep here nights from now on, and I don't think it would be very smart of you to try any tricks."

"Ha, ha," said the ghost nastily. "He who laughs last . . ."

"Ha, ha, yourself," said Jimmy's voice from close behind him. "And that's me, laughing last."

The ghost muttered and vanished.

Jimmy's aunt put cotton in her ears and slept that night in the best bedroom with the light lit. The ghost screamed for a while down in the cellar, but nothing happened, so he came upstairs. He thought he would appear to her as two glaring, fiery eyes, which was one of his best tricks, but first he wanted to be sure where Jimmy was. But he couldn't find him. He hunted all over the house, and though he was invisible himself, he got more and more nervous. He kept imagining that at any moment Jimmy might jump out at him from some dark corner and scare him into fits. Finally he got so jittery that he went back to the cellar and hid in the coal bin all night.

The following days were just as bad for the ghost. Several times he tried to scare Jimmy's aunt while she was working, but she didn't scare worth a cent, and twice Jimmy managed to sneak up on him and appear suddenly with a loud yell, frightening him dreadfully. He was, I suppose, rather timid even for a ghost. He began to look quite haggard. He had several long arguments with Jimmy's aunt, in which he wept and appealed to her sympathy, but she was firm. If he wanted to live there he would have to pay rent, just like anybody else. There was the abandoned Miller farm two miles up the road. Why didn't he move there?

When the house was all in apple-pie order, Jimmy's aunt went down to the village to see a Mr. and Mrs. Whistler, who were living at the hotel because they couldn't find a house to move into. She told them about the old house, but they said, "No, thank you. We've heard about that house. It's haunted. I'll bet," they said, "you wouldn't dare spend a night there."

She told them that she had spent the last week there, but they evidently didn't believe her. So she said, "You know my nephew, Jimmy. He's twelve years old. I am so sure that the house is not haunted that, if you want to rent it, I will let Jimmy stay there with you every night until you are sure everything is all right."

"Ha!" said Mr. Whistler. "The boy won't do it. He's got more sense."

So they sent for Jimmy. "Why, I've spent the last week there," he said. "Sure I'd just as soon."

But the Whistlers still refused.

So Jimmy's aunt went around and told a lot of the village people about their talk, and everybody made so much fun of the Whistlers for being afraid, when a twelve-year-old boy wasn't, that they were ashamed, and said they would rent it. So they moved in.

Jimmy stayed there for a week, but he saw nothing of the ghost. And then one day one of the boys in his grade told him that somebody had seen a ghost up at the Miller farm. So Jimmy knew the ghost had taken his aunt's advice.

A day or two later he walked up to the Miller farm. There was no front door and he walked right in. There was some groaning and thumping upstairs, and then after a minute the ghost came floating down.

"Oh, it's you!" he said. "Goodness sakes, boy, can't you leave me in peace?"

Jimmy said he'd just come up to see how he was getting along.

"Getting along fine," said the ghost. "From my point of view it's a very desirable property. Peaceful. Quiet. Nobody playing silly tricks."

"Well," said Jimmy, "I won't bother you if you don't bother the Whistlers. But if you come back there . . ."

"Don't worry," said the ghost.

So with the rent money, Jimmy and his aunt had a much easier life. They went to the movies sometimes twice a week, and Jimmy had all new clothes, and on Thanksgiving, for the first time in his life, Jimmy had a turkey.

Once a week he would go up to the Miller farm to see the ghost and they got to be very good friends. The ghost even came down to the Thanksgiving dinner, though of course he couldn't eat much. He seemed to enjoy the warmth of the house and he was in a very good humor. He taught Jimmy several more tricks. The best one was how to glare with fiery eyes, which was useful later on when Jimmy became a doctor and had to look down people's throats to see if their tonsils ought to come out. He was really a pretty good fellow as ghosts go, and Jimmy's aunt got quite fond of him herself.

When the real winter weather began, she even used to worry about him a lot, because, of course, there was no heat in the Miller place and the doors and windows didn't amount to much and there was hardly any roof. The ghost tried to explain to her that the heat and cold didn't bother ghosts at all.

"Maybe not," she said, "but just the same, it can't be very

pleasant." And when he accepted their invitation for Christmas dinner she knitted some red woolen slippers, and he was so pleased that he broke down and cried. And that made Jimmy's aunt so happy, she broke down and cried.

Jimmy didn't cry, but he said, "Aunt Mary, don't you think it would be nice if the ghost came down and lived with us this winter?"

"I would feel very much better about him if he did," she said.

So he stayed with them that winter, and then he just stayed on, and it must have been a peaceful place for the last I heard he was still there.

THE MYSTERY
OF RABBIT RUN

JACK BECHDOLT

Three young travelers in single file plodded through midsummer heat, crossing the bridge between Lambertville, which is in New Jersey, and the village of New Hope, in Pennsylvania.

John Carpenter led the way. John was nearing twelve years—lean, wiry, and tall for his age. Behind him, close enough to carry on a conversation, came his sister Madge. Madge was ten, with a mop of red-brown hair on her shoulders.

Behind these two—and a long way behind—was Oliver Mead, their cousin, a spindly boy of eight years, his thin little body pulled awry by the weight of an oversize suitcase, his red, perspiring face set in lines of desperation as he struggled to keep up. His glasses were so steamed over that frequently he blundered into the iron guard rail of the bridge.

Unlike his two older cousins, Oliver had never before been invited to Rabbit Run, a country place in Pennsylvania owned by their Aunt Judith. It had been carefully explained to him by Mother that they would be met by Captain Ben, the caretaker, and the Rabbit Run station wagon at Lambertville.

But they hadn't been met. They had waited an hour. When there was still no sign or word of Captain Ben, John had desperately canvassed their joint finances to see if they could afford a taxi. John had eighty-nine cents. Madge had twenty-six cents. Oliver had nothing. Mother had forgotten to give him pocket money in the flurry of their departure from Pennsylvania Station in New York.

Oliver had been terribly embarrassed. They couldn't hire a taxi to carry them all the way to Rabbit Run with one dollar and fifteen cents. That was when John picked up his battered canvas zipper bag and announced they would have to walk it.

John glanced upriver and frowned. In the northeast great thunderheads rolled up. The wooded shores of the lovely valley looked ghastly green under a strange half light. Beneath a blackening sky the Delaware River flowed smoothly, like a sheet of highly polished pewter.

A three-mile hike to Rabbit Run, thought John. He and Madge were all right. Madge was pretty nearly as hardy as he was. Rain wouldn't hurt her. But Oliver!

Oliver never went within a mile of poison oak but he came down with spots and swellings. Oliver was beloved by every mosquito and poisonous insect known to the books.

John paused to look at the struggling little figure with the big bag and Oliver, taking the halt as a warning speeded up his staggering legs. That was the worst of Oliver—he was so anxious to please and so embarrassingly in awe of his cousins.

"Oliver, the Drip," Madge called him, and how well it fitted!

"Here," said John impatiently, and snatched the bulging suitcase from Oliver's hand. "You carry my bag; it's lighter. What's in here anyhow?"

Oliver blushed deeper red. "Things," he piped. "Things Mother said I would need for a week in the country. You know, like extra shoes and things. I'm afraid you'll find it awfully heavy."

John had already found that out. "We've got to keep pushing right along," he exclaimed. "But you sing out if we set the pace too fast."

On through New Hope they pushed, without a pause to admire the old stone houses and the giant shade trees. Up the rise in the Philadelphia road, and then down steps to follow the towpath along the canal.

Every step of the way had happy memories for John and his sister. They had spent many summer vacations at Rabbit Run. The towpath was a reminder of the picturesque days when the canal had been filled with water and constantly ruffled by the mule-drawn boats laden with coal from the Pennsylvania mines.

Old Captain Ben had told them about all that ever since they'd been old enough to listen. Captain Ben once had commanded a mule and a canal boat himself. Now the canal was empty for stretches, half filled with muddy water in others. Its weed-grown locks stood with big gates ajar. The bones of old canal boats baked white in the mud.

In spite of John's good resolution, his footsteps quickened and he and his sister drew away from Oliver, far enough so that Madge felt free to make a woeful face and sigh, "It isn't fair, making us bring him along. It was *our* vacation, and we were going to have such a glorious time exploring and fishing!"

"Aw, it'll be all right," John muttered. "Look, Corabel will be at the farm. Well, she can look after Oliver. He'll give her enough to do so she won't be lecturing us all the time."

Corabel was Captain Ben's daughter and housekeeper. When John and Madge were very young she had been employed as a maid at their house and she still assumed all the authority of a parent.

Madge smiled. "Oh, John, can't you see her fishing him out of poison ivy and patching up his bee stings! That's a lovely thought."

They pushed on, straining their eyes to see which would be first to spy the farm. Madge won, pointing out the two big stone chimneys just visible above the forest. As if her raised arm had been a signal, the mutter of distant thunder stopped abruptly. The whole world was quiet, listening, shivering with anticipation. Gray storm wrack was obscuring the thunderheads.

"We're going to catch it," John said.

Rabbit Run Farm lay in a strip of fertile bottom land between the old canal and the river. Where the private road crossed the tow-path on a bridge, they paused to check on Oliver.

He was limping. Even John's light zipper bag seemed to weigh him down, but his piping voice came clearly in the unnatural hush.

"Don't wait. I'm all right. Get in out of the rain."

They sighed. And waited.

For about a quarter mile the private road ran through forest. It was almost like a tunnel in the murky light of the gathering storm.

At the bend, where you got your first clear view of the old farm-house, they paused again, as had always been their habit.

Seen through a vista of thick timber, Rabbit Run gleamed ghostly in the queer light. Its center wing, the original stone house, stood three stories, with narrow windows sunk in the thick walls. The line had been softened by the addition of two lower wings, one on either side of the original. A stranger, seeing it for the first time, overshadowed by trees in the thickest of summer foliage, might have thought it a little lonesome and a little grim.

Suddenly they heard the violent crackling of underbrush. Some-body or something was moving through the wood close beside them, jumping logs, charging through thickets.

A little startled, John shouted. There was no answer.

"Funny," he said. "There certainly must be somebody there."

Oliver said a little unsteadily, "I have read that the cougar, or mountain lion, often follows travelers, keeping hidden in the woods."

Madge squealed with joyous laughter and John grinned.

"No mountain lions around here, Oliver. No mountains, either."

"It was in a very good book on natural history that Mother gave me for my birthday," Oliver's eyes were round, his lips trembling.

Then the rain fell suddenly, like a torrent, and they had more pressing things to think about. But afterward, after stranger and more serious happenings at Rabbit Run, they remembered that incident as the start of their adventures.

The kitchen was the place to find Captain Ben and Corabel, and that was the door they raced for. The upper half of the Dutch door stood open and electric lights made the room bright, but their shouts went unanswered. Nobody was in the kitchen; nobody was in the house, as they soon learned.

The rain was sluicing down, making noise enough to cause them to raise their voices.

"Ben must have started to meet us and got a flat tire," John thought.

"He can't have, John." Madge drew her brother to the door and pointed. "Look, the garage door's open and the station wagon's inside."

"He and Corabel are in the barn, keeping dry," John guessed again. Later they were to know that John was mistaken.

Oliver had been staring about. "I didn't know Aunt Judith kept a dog," he murmured.

"Dog?" said John. "She doesn't. Ben doesn't either."

Oliver was on all fours, peering nearsightedly at the floor.

"Those are dog tracks," he insisted.

There were pawmarks on the scrubbed pine planks, and they looked decidedly doggish.

"Yes, and somebody's been eating a meal," said Madge, pointing to the corner of the kitchen table. She picked up a cup half-filled with coffee. The coffee was still warm.

"He got out of here in a hurry, too," John contributed. "Knocked over his chair, he was in such a rush. And threw his napkin on the floor. Never knew Captain Ben to do that. He's neat, even when he hurries. And as for Corabel, she'd die sooner than not put her napkin in her napkin ring."

There was uneasiness in John's voice, in spite of his attempt to seem casual. Oliver's eyes grew wider. He began to think Rabbit Run a strange and unfriendly place.

Oliver felt twitchy and crawly. He shivered. He sneezed. It was a big sneeze for a small boy and it startled them like a pistol shot.

Madge took charge with firm hand. "John, take him to your room and make him change every stitch he's got on. And Oliver, you wear your sweater, even if it is hot in here."

Madge had cleared the kitchen table and set three places when they returned. She was rummaging in the electric icebox that was Corabel's pride.

The rain was letting up. John went to the barn to look for fresh eggs—it was then he learned positively that neither Captain Ben nor his daughter was there—and Oliver was set to work tidying up the room. Oliver's activity led to the discovery of the telegram—their own, sent that morning from New York, telling the time of their arrival.

"It was back of that stove leg," Oliver reported. "All crumpled up, as if somebody had thrown it there. It's kind of funny, isn't it?"

"Shucks," said John. "Nothing funny about that." But it was rather odd, and he kept puzzling over it.

Darkness had fallen long before supper was ready, and before the dishes were done, the storm was back again from a different quarter, bringing another heavy rain and a high wind that made the elms and buttonwoods about the house thrash their branches.

For all John and Madge could do, a general feeling of uneasiness prevailed.

"We'll build a fine big fire in the living room," John decided. They moved into the paneled, lovely room that Aunt Judith had contrived by tearing out partition walls. A fire was laid ready on the old brick hearth, but John could not find any matches.

"I'll get them," Oliver volunteered. "There's a boxful in the kitchen."

"I can't figure out where Captain Ben and Corabel went," John puzzled. "That telegram got here. He knew we were coming. . . ."

Madge's brows puckered. "If Corabel doesn't come back—and Captain Ben—we may have to end our holiday before it even begins! Maybe our folks'll let us stay here alone, but Aunt Mabel'd have a fit if Oliver . . ."

The door burst open and Oliver rushed in, his eyes big dark marbles in a white face.

"The window," he gasped. "He—it—it's staring in the window!"

John's own insides seemed to freeze up. The immediate effect of his fright was a burst of indignation.

"WHAT is? WHO is? Stop acting like an idiot."

"Yes, sir," said Oliver in a painful whisper. "But it *is*—looking in the window, I mean—a shining wet face, like—like a drowned man."

John knew it was up to him to find out what had scared Oliver, but at that moment he had no wish to see what was staring through the kitchen window. It was hard to make himself move in that direction.

He was still hesitating—and feeling decidedly uncomfortable when the kitchen outer door burst open and a hearty voice boomed out, "Anybody t'home?"

Madge gave a delighted scream, "Captain Ben!" She darted past John into the kitchen.

John turned to Oliver, his grin broad. "You little chump, you saw Captain Ben."

Madge was already clinging to the arm of a big gray-haired, whiskered man in a plaid mackinaw. John pumped his hand.

Ben Lewis' presence, his hearty laugh, his plain speech, and good common sense were better than a fine open fire to restore things to normal.

"Corabel will be madder'n a wet hen to miss you," he was saying. "She was called over to her sister's in Doylestown. They got a new baby there. What gets me is why in the name of marvel your Aunt Judith didn't telegraph me you'd started. I'd have met you at Lambertville."

The three visitors exchanged startled looks.

"But she did!" Madge cried. "Oliver found the message on the floor."

And all three launched into an account of their arrival.

Captain Ben's jaw dropped. His mouth remained open as he stared at the yellow telegraph form and heard the story. It was Oliver's contribution that produced the strongest effect of all, making Captain Ben stiffen visibly and tying his tongue for some minutes.

"Then it wasn't your dog, sir?" Oliver said.

"Dog?" Captain Ben's voice boomed.

"There were muddy paws all over the floor, sir. I cleaned them up."

Captain Ben followed his pointing finger, his scowl so intense he seemed to be willing the vanished tracks to reappear. Finally he said, "There's no dog here. Don't keep one. I've been gone since noon seein' about borrowin' the use of a tractor for a couple of days. I didn't leave any dishes and I didn't see any dog. That's got me beat."

The puzzled silence lasted several minutes. Then Captain Ben's brow cleared.

"Tell you what I think," he began. "You know how neighbors are in the country? If you're not home, they make free, knowing they'd be welcome. Somebody stopped in to pass the time of day this afternoon. I wasn't home, so he made himself a pot of coffee and had a snack. Maybe he got the telegram from the boy that delivers 'em. Probably figured he'd better read it and see if it was important. All of a sudden the thunder lets go—it's been raisin' hob all afternoon. Up he jumps. 'Gee whillikens,' he says, 'I've got to burn the wind home and get the cattle in!' And out he goes with a bang!"

His glance traveled from one face to another. His smile broadened.

He nodded. "Yessir, that's how it must have been!"

John found himself breathing a deep sigh of relief. Everything

seemed normal now. Madge was smiling. Oliver alone looked grave, but then Oliver always looked grave.

"Tell you what," Captain Ben said. "Corabel left a couple of mighty fine apple pies in the icebox. Reckon you kids could help me eat one?"

John and Oliver shared a room with two cots. As he undressed, John grinned at his cousin, "Don't you see any more ghosts tonight. That was funny, your taking Captain Ben for one."

"Yes it was," said Oliver and his voice sounded queer. "Only it wasn't Captain Ben looked in the window."

"It wasn't Captain Ben?"

"I am certain," said Oliver. "The face that was against the glass didn't have any whiskers, and Captain Ben has. It was smooth shaven, with an awful scar that twisted up on one side. And it was not Captain Ben."

John told himself that Oliver must be mistaken. Oliver was a little boy, and in a strange place, and of course he would be easily frightened. Of course the face at the window must have been Captain Ben's. But—supposing it wasn't? Supposing even that Captain Ben had been eating that meal just before they came. The coffee was warm when they found it! And suppose he had thrown their telegram away in a great hurry. And suppose there had been a dog in the kitchen. What did it mean?

"We'll get in a hike this afternoon," John said to his sister next morning. "Remember the old stone mill we were going to look up and never did? What do you say we start with that?"

"How about Oliver?" said Madge.

"He could stay with Captain Ben. We'll show him the farm this morning. That ought to hold him for a while."

Oliver was duly shown over the farm, which was less a farm than a city woman's country home. But it had pigs, chickens, and some sheep to crop the lawn, and there was a skiff moored along the river bank.

Afternoon brought an annoying change of plan. Captain Ben

was not going to be on the place, he told them at lunch. Oliver could not be left all alone, unused as he was to the country.

"You'll have to let him tag along," Captain Ben said. "Can't risk his gettin' into trouble. But cheer up. Corabel ought to be back from her sister's sometime tomorrow. She can ride herd on young Oliver after that."

After the mysteries and alarms of the evening before, things seemed very cheerful now. The day had started with bright sun and though the afternoon brought back oppressive heat and some thunderheads, the storm was not imminent. Even Oliver's presence and the possibility of his collecting bee stings, sunburn, or even broken limbs did not depress the young Carpenters.

Once again they followed the canal, closed in by forest on either side. Frequently they halted to recognize familiar places. Here was where the big kingfisher lived, and sure enough, the kingfisher, or one of his descendants, was still perched in a dead tree, scanning the quiet water for tidbits. Here was where they had found the finest spring crops of wild strawberries. It was long past strawberry time now, but worth remembering. Every turn of the canal, every landmark had its reminder of other holidays.

Oliver kept pace with them manfully, though John had secret misgivings about his brand-new city shoes. They were even rather glad they had brought him along; he made a fresh audience for their stories of adventure.

The ruined stone mill they were heading for was a little way back from the canal, entirely hidden in a rank growth of trees, creepers, and underbrush. Only by lucky accident, while following the trace of an abandoned road, had they come upon it last summer. That had been as evening was drawing in, and they had had only time to revel in its romantic gloom and make a vow to return.

At one time, as John explained to Oliver, the district had been dotted with factories of various sorts, operated by water power from the abundant streams. The canals had provided cheap transportation until railroad competition took the freight from the canals and steam or electric power made other locations more desirable. Finally, the mills, built of solid native stone, were abandoned.

"This one's a beauty," John promised. "Looks as big as a castle, and all ruins. It's kind of a scary place."

Rounding a bend in the old road they saw it suddenly, stone walls gleaming in the murk of a deep ravine. The building stood on a steep hillside, five stories in height. It was approached by a ruined bridge.

Long ago most of the roof had collapsed. Walls leaned at drunken angles and great splits in the masonry suggested imminent danger of further collapse. In the lowest level were the ruins of a flume that had carried the rushing water to primitive turbines. Now it was a broken ditch ending in a dark, overgrown tunnel.

Through all the ruin, sprouting out of cellars, thrusting their limbs through broken floors, grew lusty young trees; squirrels chattered and scuttled; birds swooped through the open roof.

John and Madge gazed entranced, like explorers who have found a new Aztec city. Oliver was silent. The place frightened him. Who knew what dreadful secrets might be hiding under those broken arches? The trickle of water through the old flume line fell into some deeper well or pond with a hollow splash that he did not like at all.

But when John said, "Come on, we'll explore," and started through the vines and brush down the hill, Oliver gritted his teeth and followed.

Some previous fall of masonry had carried away most of the bridge except the foundation of square-hewn beams. Below these was a drop of some thirty feet. Oliver saw that Madge and John proposed to walk one of those beams across the chasm, and suddenly his knees turned weak.

Madge danced along behind John, singing "The daring young man on the flying trapeze." Oliver set one hesitating foot on the square beam. More than anything, he wanted to say, then and there, "I'm scared. I can't."

John and Madge would never again have any time for him, if

he turned yellow now! On the other hand, there was his dread that he would topple off that beam into unknown depths.

Oliver was spared the decision. While he hesitated, one foot on the beam, there came a shout that made them all jump.

"Come back, you young devils! John, Madge—get out of there and come a-runnin'. You want I should paddle the pair of you?" That was Captain Ben's voice, and Captain Ben was speaking with a rage almost hysterical. They saw him on the road above, red of face and running toward them.

All three stood petrified, but a second roar from Captain Ben caused John to shrug his shoulders and return across the gap, followed by his sister.

Ignoring Oliver, Captain Ben waited on the slope, his big chest heaving, his eyes wild. He spoke again, shakily, "Of all the dumb-headed, blame fool ideas—of all the goggle-eyed craziness . . ." Words failed him. He saw the amazement in three pairs of eyes, and made an effort to speak more calmly.

"Now lookee! I'm responsible for your three young lives and limbs. Right now that place is dangerous, and if you'd get hurt in there your aunt'd fire me off my job so fast it'd make a cat dizzy. Remember now, so long as I've got to drive you three young loons single-handed, this here mill is out of bounds."

John returned his angry gaze. He said calmly, "OK, Captain Ben. You don't have to shout."

"Then come on," growled Captain Ben, and began to lead the way up the bank. He took them back over the trail and several times he broke into angry fragments of speech. At the towpath he dismissed them. "You've got the whole state of Pennsylvania to have a good time in," he said with more dignity. "But in the name of goodness, don't scare me like that again!"

When he was out of sight John shook his head in bewilderment. "I never saw him that way before—really scared, I mean. And he sure was scared! That isn't like Captain Ben at all!"

Captain Ben's behavior had put a damper on the afternoon's explorations. In spite of themselves, they talked of little else. But when they turned to the farm through a flurry of rain and wind at evening, they got a very different reception.

The kitchen was lighted and warm. Captain Ben was beaming. "Got you a real bang-up chicken-and-biscuit supper," he announced. "Corabel, she thinks she's some cook, but her old man can rustle up a meal that'd put her in the shade. Hurry up and scrub now; it's all ready to dish up!"

They discussed the change in whispers before returning, cleaned up for supper.

"I think," said Oliver, "that he's sorry for losing his temper and is trying to make up to us."

It looked even more that way when, after the dishes were done, Captain Ben kindled a fire in the living room and suggested they pop some corn.

The wind and rain were boisterous again, and it was snug by the open fire. A few leading questions from John started Captain Ben talking about canal-boat life in the old days. John and Madge had heard many of his tales of odd characters and happenings before, but they loved to hear them again and again. And tonight there was Oliver, to whom all this lore was new.

The fire was dying and it was nearly time for bed, when Captain Ben said, "I ever tell you about Peg-leg Swanson, the pirate?"

"A pirate? On a canal?" John exclaimed.

"Sure, a pirate. Anyhow, about as tough an old crook as ever throttled innocent canal skippers and robbed their widows and orphans. This Peg-leg was a terror and they say his ghost can be seen on a dark night, still steerin' his scow up and down the ditch, shoutin' curses at his poor old bony mule and roarin' out his drunken songs."

Captain Ben paused to relish their eager attention.

"Peg-leg was a deserter from a Pennsylvania regiment in the Civil War. He came here when times was boomin' and a lot of travelers carried their money with 'em, not like today when they keep it in banks." His voice sank dramatically, "And let me tell you, a lot of those travelers that encountered Peg-leg never was seen alive again."

The boughs of a big elm outside rubbed together with a screech. They all jumped.

"Stead of moorin' nights in a village, like the other boats, Peg-leg would tie up on a long reach," Captain Ben went on. "That way he would be free to prowl the roads in the dark. He had a dog, too, Peg-leg did. They tell that the dog was more murderous than his master."

Oliver piped up. "And did the law never catch up with him, sir?"

Captain Ben considered.

"Well, now!" he exclaimed. "That's the funny thing. The sheriff of Bucks County set out with his men to arrest Peg-leg one night. They had enough evidence to hang him, folks say. And do you know what?"

"What?" they demanded as Captain Ben paused again, his brow furrowed.

"He vanished! Yes, sir, just clean evaporated into thin air, him and his savage dog and the whole caboodle. They never found hide nor hair of him since that night!"

Madge's look silently questioned John. John's left eye winked significantly. It said, plain as words, "He's making up the whole story."

Brother and sister relaxed. They were sure now that Captain Ben, for some reason of his own, was trying to scare them.

If they didn't believe, Oliver at least seemed to. "Did you say, sir, that you have seen his ghost?"

W-e-e-e-ll, no—not with my own eyes," said Captain Ben. "But lots of other folks have. They report seein' the old *Myrtie Simmons*—that was Peg-leg's boat—towin' down the canal with that old rip aboard her stumpin' up and down the deck and cursin' his poor old rack-bones of a mule. The dog's with him, too, but the whole picture has kind of a queer, crawly blue light about it, like wet matches glowin' in the dark. And you can hear that wooden leg of his goin', thump—*thump!*"

As he said it, Captain Ben thumped with a log of firewood against the wide old planks of the floor. The unexpected sound made them jump.

"Funny thing, too," Captain Ben added. "That ghost outfit is always seen at the same place along the ditch, *right alongside that old mill where I met you young ones today.*"

"He's trying to scare us," John said as they started upstairs to bed. "He's trying to scare us from going near that old mill again."

Several hours later Oliver waked suddenly. He had a creepy feeling along his spine. The wind was up. But he was listening for something else, the thing that had waked him.

That was it! The sound had come from downstairs in the kitchen.

Something strange was walking about, something that walked with a shuffling, steady thump—thump—thump! Something that moved exactly as Captain Ben described the ghost of Peg-leg Swanson!

For several minutes Oliver could do nothing. He just lay still, listening.

Across the room John tossed in his sleep and began to mutter. That broke the spell. Oliver jumped out of bed and ran to John's cot. "Wake up! Please wake up, John!"

John sat up suddenly. "Is it a fire?"

"Don't shout. It's downstairs in the kitchen! It's got a peg leg. Listen!"

From the kitchen came the unmistakable thump—thump and a muttering voice.

"Hold everything," said John and swung his legs out of bed. "We'd better see if Madge is all right."

They shrugged on their bathrobes and started across the hall for Madge's room. Her door opened before they reached it.

"What is it?" she whispered.

"We'll get Captain Ben," John said. The three hurried to Captain Ben's room, their soft-soled slippers soundless on the plank floor.

There was no answer to their cautious calls. When they pushed open the door they found the room empty.

The muttering was still going on downstairs. The peg leg thump—thumped again.

"I'm going to have a look down there," John said. They went in a body down the stairs, pausing several times to listen. The sounds had ceased.

The weird howl of a dog broke the silence. The noise came from far away and ended abruptly, as if hands had caught the beast by the throat. Then there was no sound except the monotonous spatter of rain into a rain barrel.

Cautiously John unlatched the door. He opened it a crack, then wider. The kitchen was dark. When he clicked the light switch, the room was empty.

"Well, it's somewhere in the house," John said. "At least it *was*. I heard it—we all did. There's something going on around here that we ought to know about."

"I wish Captain Ben was here," Madge shivered.

"Yes, and that's queer, too," John frowned. "I can't make out what Captain Ben is up to! One minute he's nice as pie, and the next he's giving us fits for just looking at an old mill."

Oliver's voice wavered slightly, but he said what all were thinking, "Hadn't we better go over the whole house and see if everything's all right? I mean if there is . . . *somebody* . . ." Words failed him, but they knew that by "somebody" he meant a ghostly canalboat pirate with a peg leg.

John agreed that it must be done. "But stick together," he said. "No getting separated. I don't believe there's anybody around, but I don't like it. First we'll get my flashlight."

"There's a bag of Aunt Judith's golf clubs in the hall," Madge suggested.

"You and Oliver each take one," John said promptly. "We might as well be prepared."

They got the flashlight and the golf clubs and began the search on the ground floor. Familiar objects looked strange in the beam of John's electric torch and shadows moved unexpectedly. But as they snapped on electric lights, they took heart. There was nothing misplaced, no sign of any intruder.

They went up the front stairs into the dark upper hall and began with the rooms there. There was Aunt Judith's sitting room-bedroom, looking spic and span and ready for her return. And Captain Ben's room with the undisturbed bed, a bathroom, and their own two bedrooms.

They had just made sure of the boys' room and returned to the hall when the hall light, an unshaded globe in the ceiling, dimmed, gave off a strange *sizzing* sound and blacked out.

Madge jumped and clutched John's arm. Oliver gasped for breath.

"It just burned out," John said. "I noticed tonight it was an old bulb and getting dim. Let's have a look at the attic and then all go to bed." But he did not sound as calm as his advice.

A narrow stair led to the attic and the light there must have burned out long ago. John shot the beam of his torch about and all three leaped back in surprise. A ghostly figure with waving arms rushed at them.

There was panic for a moment, then Madge laughed shakily. "It's just one of Corabel's old housedresses that she left on a hanger. The draft blows it around!"

"Aw, I knew that!" John muttered. "Just a dress."

"Well, it scared me," Oliver said.

They trooped down to the boys' room. John said they had better agree on a plan.

"Maybe we're crazy," he explained. "Maybe everything is all right, but we don't understand it. Anyway, I think Captain Ben is holding something back. Oliver is dead sure there was a strange man hanging around here when Captain Ben showed up last night. And there's all the other evidence. I vote that we don't say a word to him about tonight. Not until we can find out what it's all about."

"That way," said Madge, "if Captain Ben *isn't* up to something, we wouldn't ever have to hurt his feelings by letting him know we thought he was."

"And anyway, Corabel ought to be home by tomorrow," John added.

When the boys got downstairs next morning they found Madge in the living room arranging a great bowl of roses from Aunt Judith's garden. Sunlight streamed into the mellow old room, a light breeze fluttered the curtains. No hint of ghosts on such a bright morning.

"Captain Ben's back. He's getting breakfast," Madge whispered. "He says he got worried about Jean and the baby and drove over to Doylestown after we went to bed. He says he hoped he didn't wake us, stumping around the kitchen."

"That wasn't Captain Ben we heard," John said flatly. Oliver nodded his head in agreement.

"Well, anyway, he says Corabel is going to stay away another day. The baby isn't well."

"Let's not worry about things this morning," John suggested. "It's a wonderful day. Anybody want to go into town with me? I need some films."

"I do," said Madge.

"Me, too," said Oliver. "I'm not making trouble."

"No trouble at all," John assured him.

But Oliver was bound to cause trouble. The visit to New Hope was uneventful but on the way home Oliver had a hard time keeping up. The new shoes had blistered one heel badly. Finally he was obliged to stop and take it off to ease the pain. He hoped somehow to catch up with his elders before the maneuver was noticed, but John noticed and brother and sister turned back.

"Soak it in the canal," John advised. "And don't try to lace the shoe when you put it on again. Madge, we'll take the short cut back. It'll save three-quarters of a mile."

The short cut turned off from the canal, cutting straight across a big bend. It lay through several fields, a pasture and woodland.

When they reached the woodland, John stopped to stare at a NO TRESPASSING notice on a tree.

"That wasn't there last year. This place must have changed hands. Well, nobody's going to object to our crossing the land when we've got a casualty case. Come on."

They emerged from the wood after a quarter hour on a faint trail. There was a distant shout. A stocky man in a sports jacket and knickers came striding over a rise in the field. He was waving his arms.

"You're trespassing," he shouted. "Yes, you are! Don't tell me you didn't see the signs! You're deliberately trespassing on my land. I can have the law on you," he panted. "And I'm going to. Give me your names."

"Look here," John began. "My cousin has hurt his foot and . . ."

"No excuses! Your names?"

John gave them, and the irate landowner made a show of writing them in a pocket book. "Rabbit Run, you say? Aha! I'd have thought as much. Rabbit Run . . . the people that keep a savage dog . . . Well, there's a law and courts to protect a man from them."

Was this man crazy? John was beginning to think so. He spoke up. "We don't keep any dogs at Rabbit Run. There's some mistake . . ."

Oliver had been silent through the tirade. Now he advanced a step or two and blinked up at the angry red face. "I think we had better have your name, too," he said. "We don't even know that you own this land."

"Why, you impudent little puppy!"

"Your name, sir?" Oliver repeated firmly.

"All right. It's Middleston. John C. Middleston of Fairfields. Now get off my land."

They left John C. Middleston wiping his hot, red face. "A couple more remarks from you and he'd have blown up like an atomic bomb," John grinned as he led Oliver from the scene.

"Who is John C. Middleston?" John asked at lunch.

Captain Ben dropped his fork on the floor. "What's he up to now?"

John told him.

"Well," said Captain Ben, "he's a rich man from out in Indiana or some place, that's bought the old Fairfields place and is tryin' to mind the business of everybody in Bucks County. But don't you let him worry you. If he did make a trespassin' charge against you, the court would throw it out."

After lunch Madge very efficiently bandaged Oliver's heel to prevent further rubbing and loaned him a pair of her old sneakers, large but cool and comfortable. Oliver was advised to stay off his feet for the afternoon and take a nap.

It must have been an hour later when he awakened to hear John and Madge talking in Madge's room.

"It's a heaven-sent chance," Madge was saying. "Come on, John! We've got the whole afternoon free of him . . ."

"Sure of that?"

"I just looked into his room. He's sound asleep."

Lest they come again and find he wasn't, Oliver lay down hastily and closed his eyes. But he listened.

"We'll take the fish poles and go on the river," Madge was saying.

"I'll be set in five minutes," John was saying. "Got to change my clothes."

When John and Madge were gone, Oliver sat up and drove his fist into his pillow. "As if it was my fault because I'm younger than they are!" he exclaimed. "Anyway, I can do just as many things. I talked up to that bullying fat man, didn't I? I'll show John and Madge that I can do things they're scared to do. That's what! I'll do something that'll make their eyes stick out and then maybe they'll stop going around saying I'm just a drip!"

Inspiration came suddenly. Oliver sucked in his breath and wriggled with excitement. "The mystery!" he whispered. "What if I solved the mystery of the ghost of Peg-leg Swanson?" The more he thought about it, the better that seemed to suit his peculiar talents.

Who was it who had noticed dog tracks on the kitchen floor? Oliver Mead!

Who found the telegram? Detective Oliver Mead again!

And who was the first to hear the ghost in the Rabbit Run kitchen, but this same young Oliver Mead?

"That's right in my line," he mused. "I'm a quiet person and some people think I'm plain dumb, but I notice things. I've got a Reasoning Brain."

He got the pad on which he was supposed to write letters home to Mother and curled up in a chair, busy with his pencil.

At the top of the sheet he printed one word, CLUES. Beneath he made a list:

"Gosh," he said, reading over the list. "That's an awful lot of clues, but what do they mean?"

The things that had happened did not seem in any way related. They didn't make sense. He went over the list again. At Question 5, the pencil halted. The mill!

Ben was mad when he found them at the mill. Ben ordered them to stay away from there. And later, Ben told them that hair-raising ghost story.

"Suppose," Oliver whispered, "just suppose Ben knows of something in the mill. Maybe something hidden in there that he doesn't want us to find. Maybe all the money Peg-leg stole!"

The more he thought that over, the better Oliver liked his theory. And now was the time to act!

Captain Ben was not about the house when he came downstairs. Nobody saw him leave Rabbit Run and turn off at the towpath. He met nobody as he hurried toward the old mill.

In the canal the stagnant water steamed in the sunshine, and the dragonflies and midges darted and danced above it. He passed the ruin of a lock, its big gates threatening to topple off their rusted hinges. The whitening timbers of a canal boat gave him a queer feeling. This wreck might have been the *Myrtie Simmons* herself, Peg-leg's boat.

The woods, the stagnant water, the grass-grown towpath and ruined lock all were decayed, held in a spell of silence that was frightening. It was like the uncanny hush that preceded the storm the day they reached the farm.

In spite of the heat, he shivered when he reached the mill. This building, once so busy and filled with life, looked shocking in its decay. To get inside he had to cross the ruined bridge. When he realized that, Oliver was near to turning back. Only the thought of being considered a drip forced him to teeter across one of the naked beams.

He was white and gasping for breath when he reached the broken arch that once had been the main entrance on the third floor. The floors slanted crazily. Falling rocks had torn holes in them. A few wheels and pulleys remained of the original machinery.

The second floor had once been reached by a stair. A guard rail in one corner marked the stair head, but the steps ended in empty air. A ladder had been propped against the broken steps.

The ladder was built of old timbers taken from the rubbish heaps, but Oliver noticed something very interesting about it. The nails that held this ladder together were brand new!

"Somebody comes here," Oliver thought. "Why should anybody come to a place like this except to hide a secret? And I am going to find out what that secret is!" He climbed down the shaky ladder.

The floor where he was now had been divided into several rooms. In one stood a thick masonry chimney that once had risen above the factory roof. In the chimney was a blackened open hearth like a blacksmith's hearth. The room had been used for mending tools.

While he stared at the forge, out of the chimney, hollow and ghostly, came a sound, half moan, half whine. And as if this had been a signal a huge gray rat ran across his sneakers.

Oliver leaped backwards. His hand struck the chimney and tore off a brick. The planks underfoot cracked. The floor dropped from under him. He fell on his back, clutching at empty air, and slid along the tilting floor until he plunged into the cellar, landing in a pool of water waist deep.

The pit he fell into had once housed some part of the machinery and was below the level of a broken stone floor. He managed to draw himself out of it and squatted dripping, feeling tenderly of a number of bruises and abrasions.

As his eyes grew used to the dim light, Oliver made out the floor overhead and the thick stone walls of the mill. The only exit seemed to be by way of a hole in the floor above, and that was a good eight feet away. To make matters worse, something stirred in the blackness of a far corner. Two eyes, green and phosphorescent, glowed at him. Something soft and warm and fuzzy brushed against him.

"A wolf!" he thought. Then the beast whined, and a rough tongue licked his cheek.

"It's friendly . . . it's a dog!" He dared now to run his hands over the shaggy coat, estimating its height and shape. It must be a big shepherd dog. After a moment he asked, "How in the world did you get down here?"

The dog snuffled him over, then sat down with a shoulder against his, panting in a companionable way. They sat just under the jagged hole in the floor above. The light was best there. As his eyes got used to it, Oliver saw the insignia on the dog's collar—three crosses.

This dog had been in the Army!

Oliver remembered something he had read about war dogs and turned back the animal's left ear. Inside the ear was a tattoo mark, 00A0 57. That was the dog's enlistment number.

He patted the dog's head. The response was instant and frightening. The wolflike head whirled toward him, lips drawn back from white fangs that grazed his hand. That drew Oliver's attention to a scar that furrowed the thick hairs. The dog had been wounded in the head, and evidently the old scar was still sensitive. But Oliver spoke soothingly, and the animal relaxed.

Oliver's thoughts soon returned to his own plight, and he felt thoroughly frightened. How would he get out? How soon would they notice he was absent from Rabbit Run?

His ankle was stiff and shot with needles of pain. He peeled off his shoe and tried to brace the ankle, making a bandage of his handkerchief.

There seemed nothing more to do, nothing except to huddle close against the dog and watch the swift fall of night. Through the night he slept fitfully, waking often with the cold and the pain of his ankle. His one consolation was to know that the dog was still beside him. It was comforting to touch that warm, furry body.

At last he awoke to find faint, gray light sifting into his dungeon. Pale as it was, dawn brought back some hope and resolution. "There must be some way of getting out of here," Oliver muttered. "Or some way to get help!"

Another inspection of the cellar disclosed nothing new. If he escaped, it must be through the means at hand and there were no means—unless—the dog!

"He can get out if he wants to," he reasoned. "I'm sure he can. Look at those movies of Army dogs scaling high walls. There must be some way to get him to bring help!"

He could not send a note. There was nothing to write on, nor to write with. Wait, how about a token? His tennis shoe, for instance?

He offered the discarded shoe to the dog. The dog seemed to understand that. It held the shoe in its jaws and watched him expectantly.

Oliver pointed to the wall and the hole above. The dog's eyes followed the gesture. It whined.

"Go find 'em, Boy," Oliver encouraged. The only response was another nervous whine.

Oliver remembered something else, that these war dogs were trained to obey a certain code and no other. He tried vainly to remember what commands were used in the film he had seen. Perhaps if he used the right word, the dog would obey.

There was HEEL, for instance, a word that brought the dog smartly to heel, pressed against the left leg of his trainer. And SIT and DOWN, words that never varied. But what was the word that would send this highly trained animal ranging about the countryside?

John and Madge were far out on the Delaware River, near the Jersey shore, when Oliver started on his errand to the mill. The river was broad there, the current lazy, and the day was fine. Just the sort of afternoon for a holiday, when you could ship the oars and stare at the piling summer clouds and not care whether you ever caught a fish.

John sprawled with his head pillowed on a rolled-up sweater. Madge dangled her hands in the cool water from the stern. For perhaps the sixth or seventh time in the course of the last two hours she murmured:

"I'll bet Oliver forgot to change the bandage on his heel like I told him."

"Oh, suppose he did!" John sounded impatient. "What's the difference . . ."

"Well, it would be a lot of difference if his foot got infected! It would be just like him if it did. We'd catch it from Aunt Mabel, too!"

"Look here!" John said. "You've done nothing but worry about Oliver since we started. Oh, I'm not blaming you. Maybe we shouldn't have skipped off and left him alone. Want to go back now?"

"Oh, well," Madge pretended indifference. "I suppose we ought to be turning back anyway."

Their return was earlier than they intended. They found Captain Ben home. He greeted them with, "Isn't Oliver with you?"

They shook their heads.

"Then where in the nation is he?" Captain Ben sounded vexed —or worried, perhaps. "I've been going over the place with a fine-tooth comb. He's not here."

"He won't have gone far with that foot," said John. "He's sure to show up in half an hour."

Later, when supper was ready, they were not so sure. They finished the meal hurriedly.

"We'd better do a little looking around," Captain Ben announced. "We've got to find him before dark."

But they didn't find Oliver before dark. Nor after dark. The matter had now become very serious, and Captain Ben went out in the station wagon, asking questions at every farm and recruiting a search party.

John and Madge remained at Rabbit Run. They hoped for a telephone message, either from Oliver himself or from somebody who could tell where he was. They debated notifying Oliver's mother. Neither had any taste for that and they put the matter up to Captain Ben on his return.

"Wait a bit," was his advice. "No use gettin' your aunt all steamed up unless there's cause to. He can't have gone very far."

"Why did he go at all?" John burst out. "The poor little chump! He's always been that way, ever since he could crawl. Always getting into a mess!"

"If we'd only taken him with us today," Madge cried. "And that's my fault. I was the one that said to leave him home."

Captain Ben patted her shoulder. "Take it easy. We don't know that any harm's come to him. Like as not when it gets dawn, we'll find him. A dozen men have promised to help us look as soon as there's any light to see by."

"Don't you think we ought to tell the State Police?" John suggested. "They're awfully good at looking for lost people."

Surprisingly, Captain Ben's heavy brows met in a startled frown. "State Police? Nonsense!"

"But they could help us look. They—they might bring some bloodhounds and trail him."

"Yes, and tell every city newspaper from here to San Francisco! And would your Aunt Mabel have a fit then! No, sir, I—we—can handle this ourselves. And anyhow," his voice boomed with irritation, "stop actin' like Oliver's really lost. Or hurt. We haven't any proof that he's in any trouble at all!"

He got up from the kitchen table where he had been drinking hot coffee and went abruptly to the telephone in the hall. Through the door which he slammed after him, they could hear him asking for a number and then the mutter of a long conversation.

John turned to Madge in significant pantomime. They drew away to a far corner of the kitchen. "Did you notice anything funny about him?" John asked.

Madge nodded. "He doesn't want to tell the State Police."

"You know what, Madge! There *is* something queer going on around here. It began when we came. I've been thinking about Captain Ben's explanation of those dishes and the telegram. His story doesn't hold water. Even if a neighbor came in here and helped himself to a cup of coffee, can you imagine any one reading an important telegram that isn't his, and throwing it away?"

"And that business at the mill," Madge put in. "And a lot of other queer things—Oh John!" Her voice was near tears. "We always trusted Captain Ben. If we can't believe in him, what are we going to do?" They heard Captain Ben hang up the telephone and drew apart hastily.

He came back with a reassuring smile. "I called in an expert," he announced. "Fellow that knows the country like I know the back of my own hand. Shorty McGowan."

He looked at them as if he expected recognition of the name. When they returned the look blankly, Captain Ben went on. "Thought most likely you'd read about Shorty. Even the New York papers carried a piece about him the time he won the Distinguished Service Medal. He's New Hope's top hero."

"Army?" John asked politely.

"The Leathernecks. He was in all the early, big fights in the Pacific till he got a piece of Jap shell in him and they sent him home. Get him to tell you about those army dogs they trained to go out under fire and find wounded men. He's a mighty interestin' talker on that subject."

"If he knows how to find Oliver, I don't care what he talks about," Madge said.

"He will! You take my word for it. Shorty knows every foot of this country. He's hunted and fished and explored all over it. He'll find Oliver."

Neither John nor Madge could share Captain Ben's enthusiasm. His cheerfulness seemed rather forced.

"Now get off to bed," Captain Ben ordered. "I want you to get all the sleep you can. Shorty will be out here by daybreak and we'll start things humming."

Sleep seemed about the last thing they were likely to enjoy that night. From their rooms across the hall, the doors open, brother and sister talked in low tones, going over all the possibilities that might have kept Oliver from returning to the farm. How could they sleep?

And yet they did, eventually, until Captain Ben's hearty voice brought them wide awake. "Rise and shine, young ones!"

Madge leaped up, her heart beating fast. Had they found Oliver? A couple of minutes later, as they tumbled half-dressed down the kitchen stair, her heart sank again.

Captain Ben opened the door for them with the announcement, "Want you to meet a special friend of mine, Shorty McGowan. If anybody can find young Oliver, Shorty's the man."

In the kitchen sat a chunky man half Captain Ben's age. His weather-beaten, snub-nosed countenance had a reassuring smile in spite of an old scar that disfigured one cheek. He wore an odd assortment of clothing, partly the forest green uniform of the United States Marines, partly civilian.

Propped against the chair he sat in were crutches. Shorty McGowan still limped from the wound he had received at Bougainville.

The gray, reluctant light of a new day was trying ineffectually to outdo the kitchen brightness. Madge took hope. They could begin the search now! But even that logical next step seemed doomed to annoying delays.

Captain Ben said that breakfast was the first thing to attend to. He had prepared the meal before he waked them, and he insisted that John and Madge eat heartily.

The two men outlined plans as they ate sausage and eggs and hot cakes. Somebody must remain at the farm to attend the telephone and receive reports.

"Madge had better stay right here and look after that," Captain Ben said. "And keep plenty of hot coffee and grub ready."

"No!" Madge's cry was involuntary. She caught Captain Ben's arm, pleading, "Don't make me do that. I can search! I'm good in the woods! It isn't fair to make me stay here and wait!"

"Somebody has to do that," Captain Ben said kindly. "It's just as important as searching. More so. And it's up to you to take orders like a good soldier."

"He's right," John whispered to his sister. "You know he's right, Madge."

Madge was nodding, too overcome to speak, when a car appeared in the drive and from it clambered a well-remembered figure, a stoutish, motherly woman they had always known.

"Corabel!" Madge exclaimed, and flew to her old nurse.

"I just got your message about Oliver," Corabel explained to her father. "I'll take over headquarters here and you pass the word that anybody that wants it will find a hearty breakfast waiting."

"Then I can go?" Madge exclaimed, and Captain Ben nodded. "So long as you and John stick together," he agreed.

After some discussion with Shorty, Madge and John were assigned to a search of the woods on the Fairfields land, where they had had such an unpleasant interview with John C. Middleston.

"You may find Middleston himself, bumbling around there," Captain Ben said. "But he won't do any objectin' today. He's disagreeable, but he'll do his share tryin' to find Oliver all right."

"We're going that way," Shorty added. "You can come along with us and we'll drop you off."

As they bounced along in the station wagon, John asked, "You've got the old mill covered, haven't you, Captain Ben?"

Again the Captain scowled and the color mounted in his cheeks. "That's about the unlikeliest spot I can think of unless it was the planet Mars! If one of you two hellcats was lost, I'd figure on lookin' there. But Oliver's never that crazy."

"But he might . . ." John began.

Shorty intervened. "Sure, we'll search the mill. But we've got to take the nearer, likely places first. That's all Ben meant . . ."

Captain Ben, who was driving, jammed down the brake pedal and the jolt of a sudden stop interrupted Shorty. The portly form of John C. Middleston was in the middle of the road, behaving like a traffic policeman.

"Any news?" the landowner demanded.

"No news, except it's time we all got busy and did a little searchin'," Capain Ben growled.

Middleston bristled. "Oh, it's you, Ben Lewis!" He peered into the car. "And Shorty McGowan, too. Well, McGowan, if you're so anxious to be of service, you might start by telling where you hid that man-killing dog of yours."

"I might, but I'm not going to!"

The landowner's voice rose. "I demand to know where you and Ben Lewis hid that savage brute!"

Shorty's face had lost its easy smile. His eyes were small with rage. "If I did know where my dog is, I wouldn't tell you."

"And that goes for me, too," Captain Ben shouted suddenly.

Madge and John exchanged bewildered glances. What dog were they quarreling about? And anyway, why should a quarrel over a dog interrupt . . .

Impatient at this senseless delay, Madge broke in, "Stop it!"

The three men stared at her.

"Stop it, I say. I don't know what you're talking about, but you've got to forget it. The idea of wasting time over a silly quarrel when you ought to be searching for Oliver. Why, he might be dying while you fool around here talking about a dog . . ."

Madge broke off abruptly.

Over Middleston's shoulder, unnoticed by any of the others, she saw a shaggy, wolflike creature racing at top speed toward them. A dog! A big, brindle shepherd dog charging like a furry comet, headed directly toward the station wagon!

The dog shot past Middleston with a nudge that sent him staggering. It hurled itself onto the fender of the car and thrust its body half through the driver's window. It dropped something into Shorty McGowan's lap.

Middleston's voice rose, shrill with excitement. "That's the dog that attacked me. I suppose you . . ."

"Be still," Shorty snapped. Middleston was silent, staring, as they all did at the object the ex-Marine was holding up. A tennis shoe!

"That's my shoe," Madge cried. "I loaned that pair to Oliver."

"Glory be, the dog has found the boy," Captain Ben said. "All we've got to do is follow him."

Middleston's mouth hung open. His eyes bulged as he stared at the shoe. "Do you mean to say . . ."

"Of course, I do," Shorty answered. "The dog found the little boy. He's trained to bring me a token when he finds a wounded person. He's an Army dog."

Shorty's arms were about his dog as he glared at Middleston. "And that's the dog you've been yelling for us to kill. If you kill that dog, you'll have to kill me first."

Ben put the car in gear. "Turn Chang loose, Shorty. Tell him to take us to Oliver."

Shorty opened the door and gestured with outflung arms. "Chang! Search!"

The big dog was off with a bound, skimming back over the road they had just traveled, headed toward the towpath. The station wagon make a quick turn and followed after.

"Wait for me," Middleston shouted, and hurled himself onto the step.

It was not two hours later that Oliver found himself sitting at the table in the Rabbit Run kitchen, devouring the last crumbs of a big helping of country sausage.

"No more hot cakes, Corabel," he said dreamily. "But if it's not too much trouble—I mean if you happen to have any handy—I would like a piece of your apple pie."

Shorty McGowan grinned. "Guess a few hours in that cellar didn't sprain your appetite none. How's the ankle?"

"Oh, very comfortable, thank you, Shorty. I can't begin to thank you—or your dog . . ."

"You said that before," Shorty protested. "About a dozen times by my count. It was all Chang's doing, not mine. And lucky for you we picked the old mill to hide him in. And that you finally happened to give him the right command."

"If you don't mind," Oliver said politely, "that's one of the questions that has been bothering me. Why were you hiding him?

And some other things that happened right here at the farm. That telegram, for instance. And Captain Ben's not being there when we came, and . . ."

"That's Ben's yarn, not mine," Shorty grinned. "He engineered this deal. Let him tell about it."

John and Madge drew chairs closer. Corabel deposited a generous slice of pie in front of the invalid and joined the circle. "I might've known Pa would get into trouble if I left him alone here," she announced.

"I'd better begin with the beginnin'," Captain Ben said. "If there's any questions, you fire 'em as I go along. In the first place, Shorty came home from the Pacific and brought his dog that was invalided out when he was. Because the dog's got an old scar on his head and fool people want to pat him, Shorty kept him on leash, and the story got around that Chang was dangerous!"

"And he snapped at Mr. Middleston?" Madge broke in. John nudged her. "Let him tell it."

"Yep, Chang snapped at Middleston, and Middleston claimed the dog attacked him."

"Which was a lie," said Shorty.

"The court believed him, anyhow, as John and you heard, Madge. And the judge ordered the dog killed. But the dog couldn't be found."

"I smuggled him out to Rabbit Run," said Shorty. "If I kept him, sooner or later Middleston would have found it out. He was watching me."

"The afternoon you kids came," Captain Ben went on, "I was havin' a bite here in the kitchen and Chang was with me. A kid from the village brought your telegram. I couldn't let you get mixed up in somethin' pretty much like breakin' the law. I had to act fast and get that dog out of the way. You see your telegram didn't arrive till after your train time, so I barely had time to light out with the dog when you three came prancing down the road."

"It was you we heard in the brush," Oliver exclaimed.

"That's right. I took Chang over to the mill. And I phoned to

Shorty. Shorty got here at the same time I got home. I met him waiting for me in the yard because he'd seen you kids in here...."

"The face at the window!" John exclaimed.

"Then, next day," said Captain Ben, "you kids just about scared the life out of me by making a beeline for the old mill. I hadn't dreamed that would happen and I guess I sounded pretty mad."

"And that night you told us about Peg-leg Swanson, the pirate," Madge broke in. "Oh Captain Ben, was it all just made up?"

Captain Ben grinned sheepishly. "Well—I did once know a fellow called Peg-leg Swanson. He skippered a canal boat, too. But otherwise he used to take his wife and eleven tow-headed kids to church in whatever town he tied up in on a Sunday. You couldn't call him exactly a pirate. But I had to scare you away from the mill somehow!"

"It was Shorty's crutches we heard thumping in the kitchen that night," John said to Oliver.

"I came to get news of my dog," Shorty nodded. "You see, I knew he'd stay in the mill until he got orders to come out, because he's trained to do that. And I got sort of worried, thinking of him all alone out there . . ."

"But it's all right now," Madge smiled. "I never saw anybody so admiring as Mr. Middleston was when Chang led us to Oliver! I think he apologized very nicely."

Oliver startled them with a loud yawn. He had regained a good color and he looked stuffed to the limit with Corabel's hearty breakfast. "Would you all excuse me?" he asked, pushing back his chair. "I think, if nobody minds, I'd like to go to my room now and get a couple of hours' good sleep. I'd like to be in good form before we have any more excitement at Rabbit Run."

THE FORGOTTEN ISLAND

ELIZABETH COATSWORTH

The fortuneteller told them both the same fortune. Jane went into the tent first and sat there with her hand held out across a table covered with an Oriental cloth. She felt a little scared, as the woman in the bright-colored skirt and white waist, earrings, and a handkerchief about her head, looked at her palm for a while.

Then the fortuneteller said, "There is adventure ahead of you. I see it soon, and yet the adventure is connected with something from far away and long ago."

The fortuneteller said some other things, too, unimportant things that didn't stick in Jane's mind after the sound had left her ears. She paid her quarter and slipped out. John was waiting for her.

"Any good?" he asked.

"I'm not sure," said Jane. "I don't suppose she's a real gypsy."

"The money goes to charity anyhow. I'd better see what she tells me," John said, and he went in.

"What did she tell you?" Jane asked as he came out a few minutes later.

"Oh, a lot of stuff about school, and being on the football team if I only believed I could make it. A lot of stuff like that. And then she said I was to have an adventure, soon, and that it was connected with a faraway place and things that had happened a long time ago."

Jane's gray eyes flashed indignantly.

"I bet she says that to everyone! That's just what she told me. I feel like going in and asking for my quarter back."

"Hold on." John was more logical than Jane. "Maybe we might be going to have it together."

They stuck around the tent. It was part of a church affair on Mrs. Sumner's lawn, and it was made up mostly of flower and needlework booths and things like that, with a pony they felt they were too big to ride, and a grab-bag filled mostly with rubber dolls and rubber balls. After getting themselves another bag of brownies, they had plenty of time to question some of their friends who had had their fortunes told, too.

"Hi, there! Bill, what did she tell you?"

They must have asked five or six children, but to none of them had there been promised an adventure of any kind. It kept them making guesses.

"I bet she means our going up to the cabin. That's an adventure, right on Green Lake, in the woods and everything," Jane said. But John, who was two years older, twelve going on thirteen, shook his head.

"It couldn't be that, Jane," he argued. "The cabin's new. Dad just had it built last winter. And it's on land where nothing has ever been before. That couldn't be it. We'll have to wait."

"I can't bear to wait!" Jane cried.

John grinned at her.

"Don't know what you'll do about it," he said. "Come on, I've got five cents left. That'll get us a piece of fudge, anyhow."

Two weeks later the Lane family were climbing out of their car at the end of a rough Maine woodroad. For a moment they all four stood still, feeling happy. Then Mr. Lane unlocked the back of the car and they began to carry suitcases and blankets into the new log cabin which stood a little back from the edge of the water. They were as busy as four chipmunks during acorn season.

No one but Mr. Lane had ever seen the place. It was his surprise. He had been traveling up to Maine every week or two since last fall superintending the building of the cabin. It was made of peeled logs, oiled to make them stay clean and shining. It had a big living room with a boulder fireplace with a fire already laid, which Mother immediately lighted as a house warming. There was a small kitchen, too, with a sink and a new pump painted red under the window, and three bedrooms in a row opening from the big room. Out of John's room went a stair leading up into the loft where cots could be placed when the Lanes had friends.

"James," exclaimed Mrs. Lane. "You've thought of everything."

"You're pleased, Janet?" he asked anxiously. "It's the way you thought it would be?"

"Only much nicer!" said Mother.

The Lanes were a family that had very good times together. They loved to go camping together and they could all paddle and fish and swim and build a fire outdoors and flap pancakes on a skillet. So it had seemed perfect when Father found this land on a secluded cove on Green Pond and began having a cabin built. Now that he was a senior member in his law firm, he seemed able to get away from his offices a good deal in summer.

"People don't feel so quarrelsome in warm weather," he used to say—though that was probably a joke. "They get crochetty in the fall and begin to go to law about things after the first hard frosts."

Anyhow, whether he was joking or not as to the reason, Father managed to get away a good deal in the summer. Now they had a place of their own, and he and Mother were happy all day long working on the finishing touches. John and Jane tried to help, and did, too, but there were times when there was no need for them. Then they were likely to get into their bathing suits, pack a light lunch, and take to the canoe to go exploring.

They had named the canoe The Adventure because of the church fair prophecies, but for a long time their excursions were of a quiet character. Green Pond was about ten miles long, but its shore line was very uneven. Now the pond was a mile or two wide, now it narrowed to a few hundred feet, only to widen once more. Long coves indented its wooded shores, and here and there an island lay like a frigate becalmed. There were farms along the slopes in many places, but only occasionally did their hay fields stretch down to the water. More often there lay a fringe of woods or rough pastures along the lake. Sometimes, these woods were very thick, extending into the wilderness which covers Maine, the great central wilderness on which the farmlands lie like scattered patches, hardly noticeable to the eagle flying high overhead against the whiteness of the summer clouds.

There were no towns on Green Pond, no summer cottages except their own, no camps. Paddling along with silent paddles the children came upon many things, a deer drinking, or a fox slipping off into the underbush, or a fish hawk rising, its prey catching the sunlight as it dangled in those fierce claws.

They heard voices calling at the farms, usually hidden from sight, and sometimes came upon a farmer fishing toward evening after the milking was done. But the sounds which they heard most constantly were the clank-clank of cowbells and the slow notes of the thrushes. Less often, they heard sheepbells. And of course there were other birds, too, the warblers and white-throated sparrows and, above all, the big loons which seemed to like them and often appeared near them, uttering their lonely cries. But when the children paddled too close, the loons would dive and when they reappeared, it would be a long way off, to teach the young humans that they must keep their distance.

One day as they were eating their lunch on a flat rock under a pine at the opening of a small bay, a curious sound began vibrating through the air. It was hard to tell where it came from. It filled the bay and echoed back from the slopes above the trees, all the time growing louder and more and more insistent.

Jane stopped eating her sandwich.

"What's that?" she asked in a low voice. "It sort of scares me."

John squinted his eyes across the glint of water.

"It must be an outboard motor," he said. "It sounds near. We ought to see it."

But they saw nothing that day.

In the weeks which followed, however, they became acquainted with that sound. Sometimes they heard it at night, waking up to raise their heads from the pillows to listen to its passing; it sounded then as though it circled in front of their cabin, like an animal circling a fire. Sometimes they heard it by day, in the distance, and once, in a thick fog which had come in from the sea, it passed very close to them. They saw the outlines of a boat and of a figure in an old slouch hat at the stern. They waved but there was no gesture from the boat, and in a moment it was gone again. Only the coughing of the engine and the rank smell of gasoline fumes were left to stain the ghostly silver of the day.

"There's something queer about that man," said Jane. "Why don't we ever see him? And why didn't he wave to us?"

John sent the canoe ahead with a powerful stroke of his paddle.

"He probably didn't see us," he said. "I suppose he goes fishing. We just don't happen to come across him."

Jane still had her paddle trailing.

"No," she said, "it's a feeling. It's as though he were always sneaking around the lake. Whenever I hear him it scares me, but when the engine stops, it's worse. Then you don't know where he is or what he's doing. But I know he's up to no good."

"That's just because his outboard motor's old and has that stumbling sound," insisted John. "He's probably a farmer at one of the farms trying to get some bass for supper."

"He chooses very queer hours to go fishing then," Jane said unconvinced. "And I don't know when he gets his farm work done, either. You know as well as I do that there's something queer about him, John, so don't keep on pretending there isn't."

"Have it your own way, Jen," John said, not admitting anything, but a queer little cold feeling came over him, too, whenever he heard that choking splutter across the water. He, too, felt relieved when several days would go by and no sound of the outboard motor would come.

Often the children would explore the woods along the shore, following little paths or wood-roads when they saw them. One afternoon toward dusk they were going single file along a trail so faint that they were not sure it was a trail at all. Perhaps the deer used it, or a cow down to the pond-side to drink. And, yet, here and there a twig seemed to have been broken off as though by a human hand.

It was hot in the woods and the mosquitoes bothered them. Jane picked a couple of big fern leaves and they wore them upside down over their heads like caps, the green fringes protecting their necks, but even so they had to keep slapping.

"I vote we go back," said Jane at last, stopping. But John peered over her shoulder.

"There's a little cliff ahead," he said. "Let's just go that far and then we'll go back." It seemed wrong to turn around until they'd reached some sort of landmark.

So Jane brandished her pine twigs over her shoulders, slapped a mosquito on her bare knee, and started ahead.

The cliff was very pretty, its seams filled with ferns, while funguses which they called "elephants' ears" seemed to be peeling in great green-and-gray scales from the granite surfaces.

But the children had no eyes for the woods at that moment. Around the faint bend of the trail something was hanging from a high branch. Jane gave a little scream of surprise and then stood staring. For it was the carcass of a sheep, such as she had sometimes seen in a butcher's shop, but strange and terrifying to come upon here in the midst of the woods.

For once the children said nothing. They stared and stared and
then turned, and John made room for Jane to pass him and go
first, while he brought up the rear with one horrified look over his
shoulder. They crashed through the woods like two runaway colts,
and never stopped until The Adventure was well out from shore.

Then Jane heaved a great sigh. "Well!" she said.

"Well!" said John.

Their father was quite matter-of-fact about their tale.

"Probably a farmer has killed one of his sheep, and didn't have
any way of getting it up to the icehouse just then. So he may have
hung it high out of reach of foxes until he can bring down a horse

or a wheelbarrow for it."

"Dad, a horse or a wheelbarrow couldn't get to that place, and it wasn't near any sheep pasture, either," John said.

"It's the man with the outboard motor!" cried Jane.

"You're jumping to conclusions, Jen," her father declared. "You haven't an iota of evidence that would stand in court."

But after a day or two of inquiry, they heard from the postmaster at the little post office, a mile or two away on the crossroads, that several sheep and heifers had disappeared in the neighborhood during the spring and summer. Some people thought that maybe a bear had come down from the north, or worse still, a lynx. If dogs had been ruining the stock, there would probably have been more noise. People inclined to think that the killer was a bear. There had been one seen for awhile four or five years ago.

"A bear doesn't butcher his meat and hang it up in a tree," said Father, and told the postmaster where the children had seen the carcass. They felt very important for a little while and would have gone on discussing the affair, if something had not happened to put it altogether out of their minds.

About three miles from the Lane's cabin, across the pond, there was a cove lying between low marshy banks, where the swamp maples stood thick, with now and then a few pines on a knoll. The cove, too, was very shallow, choked with water plants of all sorts. Water lilies, both yellow and white, lay along the outskirts in archipelagoes of broad leaves and floating flowers. Beyond grew the pickerel weeds with their thin arrow-shaped leaves and their spikes of purple flowerlets, and there were bulrushes and joint-stem grasses through which the big-eyed dragonflies flew, like splinters of sunlight.

Several times John and Jane had forced their way for a few yards into this marine flower garden, but the canoe moved very slowly. John had to use his paddle for poling while Jane peered ahead, alert for the old submerged logs which here and there lay on the shallow bottom, the bark long since peeled away, but the white stubs of branches still thrust out to rake against the bottom of a passing boat.

They had soon turned back, until one day, when pushing in as usual among the reeds, they came upon a sort of channel leading up into the cove.

"It almost looks as though it had been made," said John, "anyhow, let's go up it."

If the channel had actually been cleared, it must have been done a long time ago, for here and there it was completely grown over and once more the reeds would close about The Adventure, scraping its sides with their rubber touch. Yet by standing upright for a moment in the bow, Jane was always able to see clear water ahead, and they would push forward into a new opening.

The cove was much longer and wider than they had dreamed. They seemed to be moving in a small separate pond surrounded by maple-covered shores; all view of Green Pond was lost now, with its slopes of farmlands and woodlands and the Canton hills along the west. The breeze was lost, too. It was very hot among the reeds, and still. There was a secret feeling, moving slowly along these hidden channels, while the dragonflies darted silently in and out among the leaves.

Deeper and deeper they went into this mysterious place and as they went they grew more and more quiet. A voice sounded out of place in this silence. First, they spoke in whispers and then scarcely spoke at all, and Jane, balancing herself at the bow when the passage was blocked, merely pointed to the clear water ahead, shading her eyes against the sun.

It seemed only natural that they should come upon something wonderful, so that they were excited but not surprised when they saw an island ahead of them. It, too, was larger than one would have expected, and rockier. There were pines on it and tumbled ledges ten or fifteen feet high. The channel led to a cove where a small beach lay between low horns of rock. At a distance it would have seemed merely another knoll in the swamplands, but it was a real island, with the water lying all about it, and the shore of the mainland still some distance away.

It seemed only part of the enchantment of the place that a

house should stand above the beach, an old-fashioned house with fretwork scrolls ornamenting its eaves, and an elaborate verandah. Time had been at work here, and it was hard to say whether the walls had been brown or red. One or two of the windows had been broken by falling branches or blundering birds, and the door stood open into the darkness of a hall.

The children exchanged one glance of awed agreement and in a moment the bow of The Adventure grated on the sand. Jane jumped to the shore and turned to pull the canoe further up the beach.

Still in silence they ran up the rotting steps, and with a last glance backward into the sunlight, stepped through the gaping door into the house.

"You never saw anything like it in your life. It was all dusty and spooky with cobwebs over everything!" said Jane several hours later.

The brother and sister were home again, and telling the story of their adventure.

"And the swallows flew out and nearly scared us to death. They had their nests on the top bookcase shelves—" added John.

"One of them flew straight at my head! I thought it was a bat and that it would get into my hair."

"And there were footstools made of elephants' feet stuffed with straw, but the rats had got at them and—"

"You've forgotten about the chairs and table made of horns, John—"

"You mean I haven't had a chance to tell about them! And there was a crocodile made of ebony inlaid with ivory—"

"Hold on! Hold on, children! Is this a dream or a new game, or what?" Father demanded.

It's all real as real as real!" the children cried. "It's the island we discovered."

"They couldn't make up a house like that," Mother said. "You know they couldn't, Jim. What else was there, children?"

"Well," began John, "there had been lion skins and zebra skins on the floor, but they were pretty well eaten up, and on each end of the mantel there was a big bronze head—"

"Of a Negro girl" interrupted Jane. "John thinks they might have been boys because their hair was short, but they looked like girls and they had necklaces around their necks and their heads were held high—"

"And there were ivory tusks coming out of their heads. They were holders for the tusks. You'd like them, Mother. And there was another statue standing in an opening in the bookcase, about three feet high, a chief or a god or something with eyes made of sea shells, and hollow."

"Yes, and tell what was written over the mantel in queer letters —you remember we learned it—'Oh, the Bight of' what was it, John?"

> *"Oh, the Bight of Benin,*
> *The Bight of Benin,*
> *One comes out*
> *Where three goes in."*

"That settles it," said Father. "You two haven't gone mad or been hypnotized or had a dream. Your evidence is too circumstantial. That's the beginning of an old sea-chanty of the African Gold Coast. What else was there in this house?"

The children stared at him, their eloquence brought to a sudden stop.

"That's about all, Dad," John said, wrinkling his forehead, trying to bring back that strange interior with its smell of dust and mice and the stirrings overhead of loose boards. How could he describe how he and Jane had clung together, their hearts hammering, tiptoeing from room to room, ready to run at a moment's notice?

They hadn't gone upstairs. Upstairs had seemed too far from the open door. No one knew where they were. There might be some mysterious person living in this house, after all. They might come face to face with him at any moment. There were ashes in the fireplace. How long would ashes last? And in the dark kitchen into which they had peered for a breathless moment, John had seen fish bones on the sink-drain and an old knife. How long would fish bones last? Who had been using that knife and how long ago?

A sudden squawk from a heron outside had raised the hair on their heads. They had catapulted toward the door and then tiptoed back into what had been the living room.

"Do you think we might take the crocodile?" Jane asked wistfully. "The rats will eat it if we leave it here."

But John had a very strong sense of law.

"We don't know who owns the house," he said. "It would just be stealing. And if the rats haven't eaten it by now, they won't eat it before we can get back." For hours the Lanes sat before their own fireplace, talking over the mysterious house and making guesses about it.

It grew darker and darker outside, but Mother forgot to start supper on the stove and everyone forgot to be hungry. Over and over the children described just where they had found the house in its own lost and secluded cove. Then they went over what they had found inside. Now and then Mother asked a question, but Father hardly said anything but sat looking into the fire, smoking his pipe. It kept going out, and had to be refilled and relighted every few minutes, so the children knew he must be very interested.

"Far away and long ago," said Jane suddenly. "This is our adventure, John."

John was about to answer when the old droning squeal of the outboard motor sounded from the darkness of the lake. Once again it moved nearer and nearer them, and once more it seemed to pass the lights of their windows only to turn and pass them again.

"There's that same fisherman," Mother said, a little uneasily.

Father went to the door.

"Ahoy, friend!" he called into the darkness. "Ahoy! Won't you come ashore and have a visit?"

The engine seemed to check for a minute as though someone were listening. Then it began to sputter and drone again with its sawmill-wheel violence and, after apparently circling them once or twice more, whined off down the pond and at last merged into silence.

"I guess he could't hear me, that old outboard of his makes such a racket," Father said as he came back from the open doorway. "Anyway, it's of no importance. It's your island that interests me. Now all I can say is that there are several little ports on the Maine coast which once carried on a regular trade with the Gold Coast in the sailing-ship days. Take Round Pond—that's only about twenty miles from here. Fifty years ago, they say it used to be full of monkeys and parrots and African gimcracks brought back by the sailors. But your house has things too fine for any ordinary sailor to bring home. And why should he build a house on an island in a pond, and then desert it, with everything in it? If he was a captain, why didn't he build a house in a seaport, the way most of them did?"

"Maybe, he didn't want people to know where he had gone," Jane suggested.

"Maybe that's it," agreed Father. "But don't you think that's a little too blood-and-thundery? He probably was just a nice old gentleman whose nephew had been on a hunting trip to Africa and brought back a few trophies for his eccentric old uncle. He kept them round for a few years, and then got tired of the place and went out to California to visit his married sister. He liked it so well that he decided to buy a house, and never bothered to send for the African stuff, which he was tired of anyhow."

John looked at his father indignantly.

"That might be it, Dad!" he exclaimed. "But how about his writing 'Oh, the Bight of Benin, the Bight of Benin'?"

"'One comes out where three goes in,'" Jane finished the quotation softly.

Father looked thoughtfully into the fire.

"Yes," he agreed, "that has the voice of adventure in it. Maybe it wasn't anyone's eccentric old uncle after all. We'll find out soon enough."

"How?" the children cried, all awake and excited once more.

"We'll go to the town clerk and see in whose name the house stands."

"Tomorrow?" begged the children.

"Tomorrow, rain or shine," said Father.

"And now," said Mother, "what about some scrambled eggs and stewed tomatoes? It's after nine."

It took old Mr. Tobin over an hour and two pairs of glasses before he found the record of the ownership of the island.

"Here it is," he said at last in some triumph. "A man named E. R. Johnson bought it from old man Deering—the Deerings still own the farm back there on the east shore—paid two hundred dollars for it. That was on April 7, 1867. I remember there was talk about him when I was a boy. But he didn't stay more than two or three years, and I thought the place had burned down or fell down long ago."

He licked his thumb and turned over more pages.

"Let's see, here's the assessment for 1877, thirty dollars—that must have been after the house was built, of course. Paid. Here's 1878, paid too, and 1879. After that it's all unpaid. In 1883 they dropped the assessment to five dollars—guess they thought the house weren't worth much by then."

He went on turning pages with interest, while the Lanes sat about him on kitchen chairs watching his every motion.

"Here's 1890. I can't find any record of an assessment at all. I guess they thought a swamp island which didn't belong to anyone weren't worth carrying in the books. Kind of forgot about her. Yes, here's 1891. No sign of her in this, either. Well, let's figure her up. Three years at thirty dollars is ninety. And seven years of five is thirty-five, add ninety, and it makes one hundred and twenty-five dollars back taxes. Anyone who wanted to pay one hundred and twenty-five dollars would own the island."

Father rose and shook hands with Mr. Tobin and thanked him for his trouble.

"We'll talk it over," he said mildly. "Nice weather we're having, but we need rain."

"My peas aren't filling out," said Mr. Tobin, "just yellowing on the vine. If we don't get a thunder-shower soon all the gardens in Maine won't be worth cussing at."

Mother couldn't stand it.

"Aren't we going to buy the island, Jim?" she asked.

But Father only looked, absent-minded.

"Have to talk it over," he repeated vaguely. "Come, children, in we get. We ought to drive to town and get provisions. Thank you, Mr. Tobin. See you later—maybe."

In the car all the Lanes began chattering at once.

"Can we have it?"

"Are you going to buy it?"

"Oh, Father, how wonderful!"

"Look here," said Father severely. "You people don't know how to act about forgotten islands. You want to keep them forgotten. Raise as little talk as you can, slip in quietly, buy them quietly, don't start a ripple on the water. You'll spoil it all if you get the whole countryside sight-seeing and carrying off souvenirs. So long as Mr. Tobin just thinks you kids have run across an old cottage on an island, which you'd like as a camping place, he'll hardly give it a thought, but you mustn't start his curiosity working."

"But you will buy it?" Jane begged.

"Of course, I will. What's more I'll buy it for you and John. You found it and it's going to be yours. What'll you name it? Adventure Island?"

"No," said John, "I like Forgotten Island better. It seems more like the Bight of Benin."

"What is a bight?" Jane asked. "I like Forgotten Island, too. Forgotten Island. It makes me feel sad and wonderful."

"A bight," said her father patiently, "is a very large bay. Benin was a great city up the river from the coast. Those bronzes must have come from there, for the Negroes of Benin were famous for their bronze work. They used to trade in slaves and were very cruel. It was an unhealthy coast for whites. They died from fever and tropical diseases."

It was not until late afternoon that the children paddled their parents over to see Forgotten Island. All was as it had been the day before, except that the thunderheads were crowding along the sky to the northwest and there was a little breeze, even across the acres of the water garden. They were lucky in finding the channel again and in managing to keep to it, with Jane as lookout. Once The Adventure rasped over a flat stone, and for a second they all thought they might be stuck there, but after a moment or two, they pushed the canoe sideways and were able to go on.

But today there was a different feeling in the air. There was a continual rustling among the maples as though they were preparing for a storm. A big turtle slid off a rock at the edge of the shore, and raised its head to stare at them as they went by. It thought itself hidden among the reeds, but they could see its horny nose and the two small bead-like eyes which watched them as intruders from its hiding place. Even the house had a more secret air about it. The door still stood open, but Jane suddenly thought of a trap, and even with her father and mother there, hung back a little before going on.

However, this curious antagonism, which all felt but no one mentioned, was not strong enough to drown their interest once the Lanes had stepped across the threshold. All that the children had remembered was true and more still. There were carvings in wood, which they had forgotten, split and stained with age. They found chief's stools upheld by grinning squat figures shaped from solid logs, and hangings of curious woven cloths on the walls. Father and Mother were as excited as the children.

"I can't believe my own eyes," Mother kept exclaiming.

Father said more than once, "Now who the dickens was this man Johnson, and where did he come from, and where did he go to?"

This day they went upstairs, testing each step carefully to make sure it would hold. There were three bedrooms on the second floor, only one fully furnished, and it did not seem to go with the rest of the house. It had a set of heavy walnut furniture and a photograph of a mountain in a gold frame. The matting on the floor smelled of mold and damp and a hornet's next hung papery and lovely from one corner of the ceiling. Not a thing in the room suggested Africa. The rats and squirrels had wrecked the old mattress for a hundred nests of their own.

"It's as though Mr. Johnson hadn't wanted to think of Africa when he went to bed," Mother said, quietly, as she looked about. "Perhaps the Bight of Benin was something he preferred to think about by daylight."

Jane was standing near the window, and happened to look out. She had a distinct feeling of seeing something move behind the bushes along the shore. But though she thought "It's a man," she really wasn't sure. Things move sometimes in the corner of your glance, half out of sight. This glimpse she had was at the very edge of her vision.

Lightning flashed in the sky, silent, without thunder, and the trees shook their leaves and shivered down all their branches. She could see nothing now but the whitening leaves. Their motion must have been what had caught her attention. She said nothing, but she was ready to go back to the new cabin, which they had built themselves, about which there was no mystery.

The lightning flashed again, brighter this time, like light on copper.

"Goodness!" exclaimed Mother. "I suppose we'd better be getting back before it rains. But I feel as though we were leaving a foreign land. I expect to see giraffes staring at us when we push off."

Halfway out of the cove a sound began at some distance.

"Thunder?" Father asked, cocking his head, but the children knew, without waiting to hear it again, that it was the sound of an old outboard motor going about its secret business.

The next day Father bought the island from back taxes and

had the deed made out to John Lane and Jane Lane. The children signed it with a sense of awe.

"Now you'll have a place you can call you own," Father said, for Mr. Tobin's benefit. "You can camp there, if you're able to find a spot where the roof doesn't leak."

"Yes, Dad," the children exclaimed dutifully, but their eyes were wild with excitement. Forgotten Island was theirs; they owned its remoteness and its mystery, or it owned them. Anyway, they were bound together for all time.

For two days the words had been going through Jane's head, day and night:

> *"Oh, the Bight of Benin,*
> *The Bight of Benin,*
> *One comes out*
> *Where three goes in."*

Every morning the verse was ringing through her mind like the echoes of a gong. It had rained during the night and the air was bright and clear this morning. She was ashamed of the oppression which had overtaken her the afternoon before on the island. The coming storm had set her to shivering like the trees, she thought, and with no more reason. Why had she imagined they were being spied on? If anyone else knew about the island wouldn't he have taken away the things long ago?

Mr. Tobin saw them to his door.

"Jo Taylor, down the pond Canton way, has lost another heifer. He went out to the pasture lot to give them their salt and he says only four came for it. He had a look around, but couldn't find a sign of her. He's going to report it. There's a man calls himself Trip Anderson came in here last March and built himself a shack on the lake. Jo's suspicious of him, but it's pretty hard to get proof."

"Has Trip Anderson got an outboard motor?" John asked, thinking of the stranger.

"Yes," said Mr. Tobin, "so they say. They don't know where it came from, either. He's taken the old boat Eb Carson used to have before he died and patched it up. Mrs. Carson says she don't grudge him the boat; it was just rotting down by the willows. No one's missed an outboard round here."

"We've been all round the lake," said Jane, "and we've never seen his shack."

"I haven't either," agreed Mr. Tobin. "Don't get down to the pond much these days, though when I was a boy I was there most of my spare time. I'm not sure as anyone's seen his place, but they know it must be there, probably back a piece from the water. He's worked some for people. Told them he was planning to bring his wife and little girl when he got settled. A lot of people think he's all right, and that if anyone's stealing stock, it's likely to be that second Grimes boy who's always been wild, or that old Nat Graham. He'd as soon take a thing as look at it—vegetables, anyhow."

That afternoon the children spent a rapturous two or three hours on Forgotten Island. Once more the place had its quiet, enchanted air. Even the house seemed to welcome them in as its owners. The swallows had left their nests and with their young were flying about outside.

Jane had brought a broom and begun the task of sweeping the living room, tying her hair up in her sweater when she saw what clouds of dust she raised. John carried out the more torn and bedraggled skins. One of the hangings on the wall was in shreds, but another had held. A zebra skin, too, was in fairly good condition. They put it in front of the hearth and John gathered enough dead wood outdoors to lay a new fire.

"I'll bring an ax next time," he said, "and we must have matches in a tin box. Jen, have you noticed? This room seems as though it belonged to an older building. It's built stronger for one thing, and the floor boards are nearly two feet wide and the ceiling is lower. I think Mr. Johnson added on the rest of the house to something which was already here."

They went about examining the place and decided that John's

guess was right. The windows in the living room had many panes, and in the other rooms they were only divided down the middle in a bleak way, and the thin boarded floors swayed under the children's weight.

"Perhaps we might get the rest torn down some day and have this for the house, with a low shingled roof. We could cook over the open fire."

"And we could have a long window seat built along one wall which we could use for cots—"

"And we'd keep the African things—"

They got very excited making their plans. All the time they were talking they worked, and by mid-afternoon the room looked very thrilling. They had rifled the other rooms for anything sound and strong, and now the old part of the house had the aspect of the sitting room of some African trader.

It was John who found the old well, while gathering deadwood for a fire. "We'll bring over a new pail and a rope," he planned. "I think the water looks perfectly good."

They had never been so excited or so happy in their lives. They could not bear to go away from their new possession, and kept returning to put a last touch here or there. At last the sun had gone down and they knew they must go home. But just then Jane discovered a mass of old rubbish behind the bronze figure standing in a sort of niche in the bookcase. It was about three feet high and not as heavy as she had supposed. She dragged at it, but she put too much strength into the effort and the thing toppled over and fell with a terrifying clang.

"Oh, dear!" cried Jane. "I hope it hasn't been dented! But wait, John, till I sweep up behind him. Then you can help me get him back in place."

The statue lay on its side where it had fallen and they could see that it was hollow. It had one hand raised above its head. Perhaps it was from inside this hand, or from some corner of the inside of the head, that the things had been jarred which they found on the floor when they started to pick it up.

Gold is gold, and does not rust, no matter how long it may lay hidden. The ring, the crude little crocodile, the bird, the thing that looked like a dwarf—all were of soft virgin gold, almost warm to the children's stroking fingers.

"Look," murmured Jane in awe, "there's gold dust on the floor, too."

The pale light faintly glittered on a haze of gold. Looking at the feet of the statue they could see now that once they must have been sealed over with metal. Someone had pried them open a long time ago, and found the statue filled with gold dust and, perhaps, other treasures like these small ones which had lain concealed.

The children looked and handled and exclaimed, scarcely able to believe their own good fortune. This was "far away and long ago" with a vengeance.

"It's getting late," John's conscience reminded him. "Mother and Dad will be sending out a search party for us soon. Let's put the treasure back where we found it and bring them over tomorrow and surprise them."

"Oh, let's take it back with us!" protested Jane. "You know, John, I've had the queerest feeling twice that we were being watched? Yesterday, when we were all here, and today after the statue fell. Something seemed to be at that window, over there behind me."

"What sort of thing, Jen?"

"I couldn't see. When I turned it was gone. I went over to the window and I couldn't see anything, either."

"Why didn't you tell me?"

"I didn't want you to call me a silly."

John went out quickly and looked under the window which Jane had pointed to. There was a rank growth of nettles there and not one had been broken.

"You've been seeing things, Jen," he declared cheerfully as he came back. "No one could have been at the window. Now be a good girl and give me the things. Good, those ought to stay put. I've used my handkerchief to help stuff them back in place. Now give me a hand at setting Mumbo Jumbo on his feet again."

All the time she was helping, Jane was protesting and arguing under her breath, but John was the leader and what he said usually went. She felt rather silly, anyway, about the things which she kept imagining that she saw.

"If they've been here safe since 1879, they can stay here a day or two longer," John declared. "Wait till you see Father's face! We'll invite them here for a picnic tomorrow and end up showing them the treasure."

Next day, however, it rained hard and the children had to swallow their impatience. They wanted their party to be perfect in every way. In the late afternoon the rain changed into a fog with a little sunlight coming through.

"Can't we go over to the island?" Jane asked.

Father went out and looked at the sky.

"The fog banks are still blowing in," he said. "Smell that sea smell that comes with them! It's likely to rain again in an hour or two."

"Well, can't John and I take a picnic lunch now and just go to Oak Point around the corner?"

"We'd better let them," said Mother. "I've never known you children to be so restless. Perhaps a little paddling and picnicking will help you."

They had almost reached the point, moving through the fog so silently that they startled their friends the loons by coming upon them before they could dive; they had almost reached the point— when they found the man with the outboard motor. Everything about the picture was gray, a shabby gray coat, and a wiry shabby figure working over the motor at the stern, with the fog dripping from the broken rim of an old hat.

"Good evening," John hailed. "Can we help you?"

The man straightened and stared at them.

"No thanks," he said then, "I'll be all right," and be bent again to his work. The children paddled on and reached the point. They had already on another day built a fireplace of big stones there and

John had brought kindling in his knapsack, so that soon the fire was crackling and the smell of frying bacon filled the air.

Jane felt uncomfortable. "He looks so kind of hungry," she whispered to John. "Go on, ask him if he won't come and eat with us."

"But " began John.

"I don't care!" Jane broke in. "I don't care what people say. Ask him or I will."

The man who called himself Trip Anderson hesitated and then finally paddled his boat into shore with a crudely whittled-down board which seemed to be his only oar. He ate at the chidren's fire hungrily but remembering his manners. He seemed like anyone who was rather down on his luck, except for the way in which he met a person's glance, staring back hard, showing a thin rim of white all around the bright blue iris of his eyes. They all talked a little about the pond and the weather. The man knew a lot about fish. It was interesting, but the children were glad when supper was over and the rain began again.

"Guess we've got to go," they said, and he stared at them with his fixed eyes which he never allowed to shift the least bit.

"Much obliged, kids," he said. "I'll do something for you some day."

They told their father and mother that evening who had been their guest and their elders approved, within reason.

During the night the wind shifted to the northwest and the day came bright and perfect. The greatest excitement reigned in the cabin until 10:30 when The Adventure, laden with passengers, baskets, and extra supplies for Forgotten Island, put out into a pond that rippled delightfully.

Father and Mother were much impressed by the changes one afternoon's hard work had made in the living room. John showed Father what the original house must have been like and he caught their enthusiasm immediately.

"It wouldn't be much of a job tearing off the 1870 part," he said.

"We might be able to sell it for old wood, or if we can't, it could be burned on the rocks. Then this would be a wonderful little place. Nothing like it anywhere in the country."

The picnic was eaten in state around the table whose legs were made of horns, while a small unneeded fire crackled in the fireplace to give an added welcome. After the baskets were packed again and the room in order, Father brought out his pipe, while Mother began to knit.

This was the moment for which the children had been waiting for nearly two days.

"Want to see something else we found?" John asked with elaborate carelessness.

Jane bounded forward to help him.

They tugged out the statue and laid it on its back, and John reached far up its depths into the hollow arm, while everyone waited breathlessly.

Jane saw the look of shock and surprise come to his face and knew what had happened before he spoke.

"Why," he said rather blankly. "They're gone, the gold things are gone. There isn't even my handkerchief there.

"Sorry Jane," he muttered to her when she ran forward to help search the crevices of the statue and she squeezed his hand hard.

"It doesn't matter a bit," she cried, bravely blinking tears from her eyes. "Think of all we have left."

They didn't talk any more about the treasure. John felt too badly about it to bear any mention of it. Jane felt badly, too, of course, but it wasn't half so hard for her as for John who had insisted upon leaving the things just where they had found them.

They all paddled home to the cabin, making occasional conversation about nothing much, and that evening Father brought out Huckleberry Finn and read for hours, not saying once that his voice was getting tired.

Mother had glanced once or twice at the clock, when they heard a car come down their road and a moment later a knock sounded at the door.

It was late for visiting in the country, and everyone looked at each other in surprise as Father went to the door. Two men stood there whom they didn't know, one of them in uniform.

"Come in," said Father. "I'm James Lane. Did you want to see me?"

The older man shook hands first. "I'm Will Deering, Mr. Lane," he explained, "from over across the pond, and this is Mr. Dexter, of the State Police."

Mr. Lane shook hands with Mr. Dexter and introduced them both to the family.

"Mr. Dexter has come up here on business," Mr. Deering explained. "There've been complaints about a man who calls himself Trip Anderson. One man's lost two heifers and another man, who has a camp over on Muscongus Pond, missed an outboard motor from his boat. They brought Mr. Dexter to me because I know the lake pretty well and had an idea of where his shanty was. I took Mr. Dexter there while he was away, and we searched it and found proof he'd been doing a lot of petty thieving hereabouts. Proof wasn't needed, because when this Anderson came back, Mr. Dexter recognized him as a fellow who'd broken jail at Thomaston a year or so ago."

"His real name is Tom Jennings," the other man broke in. "He was serving a term for armed robbery. No, he ain't got a wife, nor kids. That was just cover. He's been in and out of jail since he was sixteen."

Mother looked worried, thinking that the children had been having a picnic with such a man only the evening before. But Father knew that, somehow or other, the business must concern them, or these two men wouldn't have knocked at their door at ten o'clock at night.

"Did you wish me to identify him?" he asked, but Mr. Dexter shook his head.

"He don't need identifying," he remarked, pulling out his watch and looking at it. "By now, he's at Thomaston. But just before we took him away he said he had some things he wanted to return.

He had them hidden in the flour tin. Said he'd been using the island you've bought, but never took any of the big things because they could be spotted too easy. When you kids began to go there, he kept an eye on you. He's good at that, moves like an Indian. One day when he was hanging round he heard a crash and looked in and saw you find the gold stuff. That was more up his alley. He could melt it down and no one could ever prove anything against him."

The State Policeman fished again in his vest pocket and brought out first the dwarf, and then the bird, and then the crocodile. The ring came last. He poured them all into Jane's hand, and she quickly brought them to John.

"Think of his giving them back!" she exclaimed. "Oh, thank you for bringing them! We were so bothered when we found they were gone."

"Jennings said you were good kids and had asked him to eat with you."

"Do you want to see the things?" John asked eagerly. He took them about so that everyone might examine the little objects close at hand.

Mr. Deering held up the crocodile.

"We have one at home like this," he said, "in the old teapot, I think it is. My grandfather used to say Johnson gave it to him for boarding his horse, after he'd run out of the gold-dust quills he used to get his money from. The day he gave Grandfather the crocodile and drove off was the last time he was ever seen around here. 'I took one image from that African temple that was chuck full of gold,' he told Grandfather. 'It stands to reason the other images have gold in them. Anyway, I aim to go and see.'

"But he never came back," continued Mr. Deering. "I figure he could play a trick on the temple priests once, maybe, but next time they'd get him. We never knew where he came from, nor what vessel he took for Africa, but it wouldn't be hard to find one in those days, when there was still a good trade there. Grandfather said he had the bearing of a captain. Probably no one else ever knew that the idol he'd stolen had gold in it, and he came away here, on the quiet, where no one ever would know it. But he was a reckless spender, Grandfather said. Money just poured out of his hands while he had it, and then he started back to get more. Anyhow, he never came back."

Everyone had been listening with breathless interest.

"Why didn't your grandfather use the house on the island, or sell it?" Mr. Lane asked.

"It wasn't his," the farmer replied. "Johnson had bought the island out and out. And Grandma didn't want any of that African stuff around the place. She called it outlandish, and my mother didn't like it either. We just minded our own business and no one else but us had had direct dealings with him or knew much about the place. Every year the cove filled up more and more with pickerel weed and, pretty soon, the island and Johnson were kind of forgotten—"

"That's what we call it—Forgotten Island!" the children cried.

Mr. Deering looked at them and smiled.

"Well, it's yours now," he said. "It's nice to have neighbors on it again. Glad we found you all at home."

Everyone got up to see their visitors to the door. Mr. Deering stepped out first and, as Mr. Dexter turned to say good-by, Jane asked, "Is there anything we can do for Trip Anderson?"

The officer shook his head.

"He's all right," he said. "Don't worry about him. I guess he was getting pretty tired of his freedom. He said he'd be glad to be back where he'd be taken care of. I'll tell him you inquired."

Then the door closed behind the strangers and, a moment later, there came the roar of a self-starter. Little by little, the sound receded up the road and silence settled again in the woods, and, after a while, even the Lanes' cabin was dark and still, and the Lanes, too, were asleep. But on the mantel, in the silence broken only by the occasional calling of the loons, watched the four talismans of gold, keeping guard—the treasure of Forgotten Island, made by dark hands far away and long ago.

THE WATER GHOST
OF HARROWBY HALL

JOHN KENDRICK BANGS

The trouble with Harrowby Hall was that it was haunted, and, what was worse, the ghost did not merely appear at the bedside of a person, but remained there for one mortal hour before it disappeared.

It never appeared except on Christmas Eve, and then as the clock was striking twelve. The owners of Harrowby Hall had tried their hardest to rid themselves of the damp and dewy lady who rose up out of the best bedroom floor at midnight, but they had failed. They had tried stopping the clock, so that the ghost would not know when it was midnight; but she made her appearance just the same, and there she would stand until everything about her was thoroughly soaked.

Then the owners of Harrowby Hall closed up every crack in the floor with hemp, and over this were placed layers of tar and canvas; the walls were made waterproof, and the doors and windows likewise, in the hope that the lady would find it difficult to leak into the room, but even this did no good.

The following Christmas Eve she appeared as promptly as before, and frightened the guest of the room quite out of his senses by sitting down beside him, and gazing with her cavernous blue eyes into his. In her long, bony fingers bits of dripping seaweed were entwined, the ends hanging down, and these ends she drew across his forehead until he fainted away. He was found unconscious in his bed the next morning, simply saturated with seawater and fright.

The next year the master of Harrowby Hall decided not to have the best spare bedroom opened at all, but the ghost appeared as usual in the room—that is, it was supposed she did, for the hangings were dripping wet the next morning. Finding no one there, she immediately set out to haunt the owner of Harrowby himself. She found him in his own cosy room, congratulating himself upon having outwitted her.

All of a sudden the curl went out of his hair, and he was as wet as if he had fallen into a rain barrel. When he saw before him the lady of the cavernous eyes and seaweed fingers he too fainted, but immediately came to, because the vast amount of water in his hair, trickling down over his face, revived him.

Now it so happened that the master of Harrowby was a brave man. He intended to find out a few things he felt he had a right to know. He would have liked to put on a dry suit of clothes first, but the ghost refused to leave him for an instant until her hour was up. In an effort to warm himself up he turned to the fire; it was an unfortunate move, because it brought the ghost directly over the fire, which immediately was extinguished.

At this he turned angrily to her, and said: "Far be it from me to be impolite to a woman, madam, but I wish you'd stop your infernal visits to this house. Go sit out on the lake, if you like that sort of thing; soak the rain barrel, if you wish; but do not come into a gentleman's house and soak him and his possessions in this way, I beg of you!"

"Henry Hartwick Oglethorpe," said the ghost, in a gurgling voice, "you don't know what you are talking about. You do not know that I am compelled to haunt this place year after year by my terrible fate. It is no pleasure for me to enter this house, and ruin everything I touch. I never aspired to be a shower bath, but it is my doom. Do you know who I am?"

"No, I don't," returned the master of Harrowby. "I should say you were the Lady of the Lake!"

"No, I am the Water Ghost of Harrowby Hall, and I have held this highly unpleasant office for two hundred years tonight."

"How the deuce did you ever come to get elected?" asked the master.

"Through a mistake," replied the specter. "I am the ghost of that fair maiden whose picture hangs over the mantelpiece in the drawing-room."

"But what made you get the house into such a spot?"

"I was not to blame, sir," returned the lady. "It was my father's fault. He built Harrowby Hall, and the room I haunt was to have been mine. My father had it furnished in pink and yellow, knowing well that blue and gray was the only combination of colors I could bear. He did it to spite me, and I refused to live in the room. Then my father said that I could live there or on the lawn, he didn't care which. That night I ran from the house and jumped over the cliff into the sea."

"That was foolish," said the master of Harrowby.

"So I've heard," returned the ghost, "but I really never realized what I was doing until after I was drowned. I had been drowned a week when a sea nymph came to me. She informed me that I was to be one of her followers, and that my doom was to haunt Harrowby Hall for one hour every Christmas Eve throughout the rest of eternity. I was to haunt that room on such Christmas Eves as I found it occupied; and if it should turn out not to be occupied, I was to spend that hour with the head of the house."

"I'll sell the place."

"That you cannot do, for then I must appear to any purchaser, and reveal to him the awful secret of the house."

"Do you mean to tell me that on every Christmas Eve that I don't happen to have somebody in that guest-chamber, you are going to haunt me wherever I may be, taking all the curl out of my hair, putting out my fire, and soaking me through to the skin?" demanded the master.

"Yes, Oglethorpe. And what is more," said the water ghost, "it doesn't make the slightest difference where you are. If I find that room empty, wherever you may be I shall douse you with my spectral pres . . ."

Here the clock struck one, and immediately the ghost faded away. It was perhaps more a trickle than a fading, but as a disappearance it was complete.

"By St. George and his Dragon!" cried the master of Harrowby, "I swear that next Christmas there'll be someone in the spare room, or I spend the night in a bathtub."

But when Christmas Eve came again the master of Harrowby was in his grave. He never recovered from the cold he caught that awful night. Harrowby Hall was closed, and the heir to the estate was in London. And there to him in his apartment came the water ghost at the appointed hour. Being younger and stronger, however, he survived the shock. Everything in his rooms was ruined—his clocks were rusted; a fine collection of watercolor drawings was entirely washed out. And because the apartments below his were drenched with water soaking through the floors, he was asked by his landlady to leave the apartment immediately.

The story of his family's ghost had gone about; no one would invite him to any party except afternoon teas and receptions, and fathers of daughters refused to allow him to remain in their houses later than eight o'clock at night.

So the heir of Harrowby Hall determined that something must be done.

The thought came to him to have the fireplace in the room

enlarged, so that the ghost would evaporate at its first appearance. But he remembered his father's experience with the fire. Then he thought of steampipes. These, he remembered, could lie hundreds of feet deep in water, and still be hot enough to drive the water away in vapor. So the haunted room was heated by steam to a withering degree.

The scheme was only partially successful. The water ghost appeared at the specified time, but hot as the room was, it shortened her visit by no more than five minutes in the hour. And during this time the young master was a nervous wreck, and the room itself was terribly cracked and warped. And worse than this, as the last drop of the water ghost was slowly sizzling itself out on the floor, she whispered that there was still plenty of water where she came from, and that next year would find her as exasperatingly saturating as ever.

It was then that, going from one extreme to the other, the heir of Harrowby hit upon the means by which the water ghost was ultimately conquered, and happiness came once more to the house of Oglethorpe.

The heir provided himself with a warm suit of fur underclothing. Wearing this with the furry side in, he placed over it a tight-fitting rubber garment like a jersey. On top of this he drew on another set of woolen underclothing, and over this was a second rubber garment like the first. Upon his head he wore a light and comfortable diving helmet; and so clad, on the following Christmas Eve he awaited the coming of his tormentor.

It was a bitterly cold night that brought to a close this twenty-fourth day of December. The air outside was still, but the temperature was below zero. Within all was quiet; the servants of Harrowby Hall awaited with beating hearts the outcome of their master's campaign against his supernatural visitor.

The master himself was lying on the bed in the haunted room, dressed as he had planned and then . . .

The clock clanged out the hour of twelve.

There was a sudden banging of doors. A blast of cold air swept through the halls. The door leading into the haunted chamber flew open, a splash was heard, and the water ghost was seen standing at the side of the heir of Harrowby. Immediately from his clothing there streamed rivulets of water, but deep down under the various garments he wore he was as dry and warm as he could have wished.

"Ha!" said the young master of Harrowby, "I'm glad to see you."

"You are the most original man I've met, if that is true," returned the ghost. "May I ask where did you get that hat?"

"Certainly, madam," returned the master, courteously. "It is a little portable observatory I had made for just such emergencies as this. But tell me, is it true that you are doomed to follow me about for one mortal hour—to stand where I stand, to sit where I sit?"

"That is my happy fate," returned the lady.

"We'll go out on the lake," said the master, starting up.

"You can't get rid of me that way," returned the ghost. "The water won't swallow me up; in fact, it will just add to my present bulk."

"Nevertheless," said the master, "we will go out on the lake."

"But my dear sir," returned the ghost, "it is fearfully cold out there. You will be frozen hard before you've been out ten minutes."

"Oh, no, I'll not," replied the master. "I am very warmly dressed. Come!" This last in a tone of command that made the ghost ripple.

And they started.

They had not gone far before the water ghost showed signs of distress.

"You walk too slowly," she said. "I am nearly frozen. I beg you, hurry!"

"I should like to oblige a lady," returned the master courteously, "but my clothes are rather heavy, and a hundred yards an hour is about my speed. Indeed, I think we had better sit down on this snowdrift, and talk matters over."

"Do not! Do not do so, I beg!" cried the ghost. "Let us move on. I feel myself growing rigid as it is. If we stop here, I shall be frozen stiff."

"That, madam," said the master slowly, seating himself on an ice cake . . . "that is why I have brought you here. We have been on this spot just ten minutes; we have fifty more. Take your time about it, madam, but freeze. That is all I ask of you."

"I cannot move my right leg now," cried the ghost, in despair, "and my overskirt is a solid sheet of ice. Oh, good, kind Mr. Oglethorpe, light a fire, and let me go free from these icy fetters."

"Never, madam. It cannot be. I have you at last."

"Alas!" cried the ghost, a tear trickling down her frozen cheek. "Help me, I beg, I congeal!"

"Congeal, madam, congeal!" returned Oglethorpe coldly. "You are drenched and have drenched me for two hundred and three years, madam. Tonight, you have had your last drench."

"Ah, but I shall thaw out again, and then you'll see. Instead of the comfortably warm, genial ghost I have been in the past, sir, I shall be ice water," cried the lady, threateningly.

"No, you won't either," returned Oglethorpe; "for when you are frozen quite stiff, I shall send you to a cold-storage warehouse, and there shall you remain an icy work of art forever more."

"But warehouses burn."

"So they do, but this warehouse cannot burn. It is made of asbestos and surrounding it are fireproof walls, and within those walls the temperature is now and shall be 416 degrees below the zero point; low enough to make an icicle of any flame in this world—or the next," the master added, with a chuckle.

"For the last time I beseech you. I would go on my knees to you, Oglethorpe, if they were not already frozen. I beg of you do not doo . . ."

Here even the words froze on the water ghost's lips and the clock struck one. There was a momentary tremor throughout the ice-bound form, and the moon, coming out from behind a cloud, shone down on the rigid figure of a beautiful woman sculptured in clear, transparent ice. There stood the ghost of Harrowby Hall, conquered by the cold, a prisoner of all time.

The heir of Harrowby had won at last, and today in a large storage house in London stands the frigid form of one who will never again flood the house of Oglethorpe with woe and sea-water.

THE RED-HEADED LEAGUE

SIR ARTHUR CONAN DOYLE

I had called upon my friend, Mr. Sherlock Holmes, one day in the autumn of last year, and found him in deep conversation with a very stout, florid-faced, elderly gentleman, with fiery red hair. With an apology for my intrusion, I was about to withdraw, when Holmes pulled me abruptly into the room and closed the door behind me.

"You could not possibly have come at a better time, my dear Watson," he said, cordially.

"I was afraid that you were engaged."

"So I am. Very much so."

"Then I can wait in the next room."

"Not at all. This gentleman, Mr. Wilson, has been my partner and helper in many of my most successful cases, and I have no doubt that he will be of the utmost use to me in yours also."

The stout gentleman half-rose from his chair and gave a bob of greeting, with a quick, little, questioning glance from his small, fat-encircled eyes.

"Try the settee," said Holmes, relapsing into his armchair and putting his fingertips together, as was his custom when in judicial moods. "I know, my dear Watson, that you share my love of all that is bizarre and outside the conventions and humdrum routine of everyday life. Now, Mr. Jabez Wilson here has been good enough to call upon me this morning and to begin a narrative which promises to be one of the most singular which I have listened to for some time.

"You have heard me remark that the strangest and most unique things are very often connected not with the larger but with the smaller crimes, and occasionally, indeed, where there is room for doubt whether any positive crime has been committed. As far as I have heard it is impossible for me to say whether the present case is an instance of crime or not, but the course of events is certainly among the most singular that I have ever listened to. Perhaps, Mr. Wilson, you would have the great kindness to recommence your narrative. I ask you, not merely because my friend Dr. Watson has not heard the opening part, but also because the peculiar nature of the story makes me anxious to have every possible detail from your lips."

The portly client puffed out his chest with an appearance of some little pride, and pulled a dirty and wrinkled newspaper from the inside pocket of his greatcoat. As he glanced down the advertisement column, with his head thrust forward, and the paper flattened out upon his knee, I took a good look at the man and endeavored, after the fashion of my companion, to read the indications which might be presented by his dress or appearance.

I did not gain very much, however, by my inspection. Our visitor bore every mark of being an average commonplace British tradesman, obese, pompous, and slow. He wore rather baggy gray shepherd's-check trousers, a not over-clean black frock coat, un-buttoned in the front, and a drab waistcoat with a heavy brassy Albert chain, and a square pierced bit of metal dangling down as an ornament. A frayed top hat and a faded brown overcoat with a wrinkled velvet collar lay upon a chair beside him. Altogether, look as I would, there was nothing remarkable about the man save his blazing red head and the expression of extreme chagrin and discontent upon his features.

Sherlock Holmes's quick eye took in my occupation, and he shook his head with a smile as he noticed my questioning glances. "Beyond the obvious facts that he has at some time done manual labor, that he takes snuff, that he is a Freemason, that he has been in China, and that he has done a considerable amount of writing lately, I can deduce nothing else."

Mr. Jabez Wilson started up in his chair, with his forefinger upon the paper, but his eyes upon my companion.

"How, in the name of good fortune, did you know all that, Mr. Holmes?" he asked. "How did you know, for example, that I did manual labor. It's as true as gospel, for I began as a ship's carpenter."

"Your hands, my dear sir. Your right hand is quite a size larger than your left. You have worked with it, and the muscles are more developed."

"Well, the snuff, then, and the Freemasonry?"

"I won't insult your intelligence by telling you how I read that, especially as, rather against the strict rules of your order, you use an arc-and-compass breastpin."

"Ah, of course, I forgot that. But the writing?"

"What else can be indicated by that right cuff so very shiny for five inches, and the left one with the smooth patch near the elbow where you rest it upon the desk."

"Well, but China?"

"The fish that you have tattooed immediately above your right wrist could only have been done in China. I have made a small study of tattoo marks and have even contributed to the literature of the subject. That trick of staining the fishes' scales a delicate pink is quite peculiar to China. When, in addition, I see a Chinese coin hanging from your watch-chain, the matter becomes even more simple."

Mr. Jabez Wilson laughed heavily. "Well, I never!" said he. "I thought at first that you had done something clever, but I see that there was nothing in it, after all."

"I begin to think, Watson," said Holmes, "that I make a mistake in explaining. Can you not find the advertisement, Mr. Wilson?"

"Yes, I have got it now," he answered, with his thick, red finger planted half-way down the column. "Here it is. This is what began it all. You just read it for yourself, sir."

I took the paper from him and read as follows:

"TO THE RED-HEADED LEAGUE: On account of the bequest of the late Ezekiah Hopkins, of Lebanon, Pa., U.S.A., there is now another vacancy open which entitles a member of the League to a salary of £4 a week for purely nominal services. All red-headed men who are sound in body and mind and above the age of twenty-one years, are eligible. Apply in person on Monday, at eleven o'clock, to Duncan Ross, at the offices of the League, 7 Pope's Court, Fleet Street."

"What on earth does this mean?" I ejaculated, after I had twice read over the extraordinary announcement.

Holmes chuckled and wriggled in his chair, as was his habit when in high spirits. "It is a little off the beaten track, isn't it?" said he. "And now, Mr. Wilson, off you go at scratch and tell us all about yourself, your household, and the effect which this advertisement had upon your fortunes. You will first make a note, doctor, of the paper and the date."

"It is *The Morning Chronicle,* of April 27, 1890. Just two months ago."

"Very good. Now, Mr. Wilson?"

"Well, it is just as I have been telling you, Mr. Sherlock Holmes," said Jabez Wilson, mopping his forehead; "I have a small pawn-broker's business at Coburg Square, near the city. It's not a very large affair, and of late years it has not done more than just give me a living. I used to be able to keep two assistants, but now I only keep one; and I would have a job to pay him, but that he is willing to come for half wages, so as to learn the business."

"What is the name of this obliging youth?" asked Sherlock Holmes.

"His name is Vincent Spaulding, and he's not such a youth, either. It's hard to say his age. I should not wish a smarter assist-ant, Mr. Holmes, and I know very well that he could better him-self and earn twice what I am able to give him. But, after all, if he is satisfied, why should I put ideas in his head?"

"Why, indeed? You seem most fortunate in having an *employe* who comes under the full market price. It is not a common exper-ience among employers in this age. I don't know that your assist-ant is not as remarkable as your advertisement."

"Oh, he has his faults, too," said Mr. Wilson. "Never was such a fellow for photography. Snapping away with a camera when he ought to be improving his mind, and then diving down into the cellar like a rabbit into its hole to develop his pictures. That is his main fault; but, on the whole, he's a good worker. There's no vice in him."

"He is still with you, I presume?"

"Yes, sir. He and a girl of fourteen, who does a bit of simple cooking and keeps the place clean—that's all I have in the house, for I am a widower and never had any family. We live very quietly, sir, the three of us; and we keep a roof over our heads and pay our debts, if we do nothing more.

"The first thing that put us out was that advertisement. Spauld-ing, he came down into the office just this day eight weeks, with this very paper in his hand, and he says,

" 'I wish to the Lord, Mr. Wilson, that I was a red-headed man.'

" 'Why that?' I asks.

" 'Why,' says he, 'here's another vacancy on the League of the Red-headed Men. It's worth quite a little fortune to any man who gets it, and I understand that there are more vacancies than there are men, so that the trustees are at their wits' end what to do with the money. If my hair would only change color, here's a nice little crib all ready for me to step into.'

" 'Why, what is it, then?' I asked. You see, Mr. Holmes, I am a very stay-at-home man, and as my business came to me instead of my having to go to it, I was often weeks on end without putting my foot over the doormat. In that way I didn't know much of what was going on outside, and I was always glad of a bit of news.

" 'Have you never heard of the League of the Red-headed Men?' he asked, with his eyes open.

" 'Never.'

" 'Why, I wonder at that, for you are eligible yourself for one of the vacancies.'

" 'And what are they worth?' I asked.

" 'Oh, merely a couple of hundred a year, but the work is slight, and it need not interfere very much with one's other occupations.'

"Well, you can easily think that that made me prick up my ears, for the business has not been overgood for some years, and an extra couple of hundred would have been very handy.

" 'Tell me all about it,' said I.

" 'Well,' said he, showing me the advertisement, 'you can see for yourself that the League has a vacancy, and there is the address where you should apply for particulars. As far as I can make out, the League was founded by an American millionaire, Ezekiah Hopkins, who was very popular in his ways. He was himself red-headed, and he had a great sympathy for all red-headed men; so when he died it was found that he had left his enormous fortune in the hands of trustees, with instructions to apply the interest to the providing of easy berths to men whose hair is of that color. From all I hear it is splendid pay and very little to do.'

" 'But,' said I, 'there would be millions of red-headed men who would apply.'

" 'Not so many as you might think,' he answered. 'You see it is really confined to Londoners and to grown men. This American had started from London when he was young, and he wanted to do the old town a good turn. Then, again, I have heard it is no use your applying if your hair is light red, or dark red, or anything but real bright, flazing, fiery red. Now, if you cared to apply, Mr. Wilson, you would just walk in; but perhaps it would hardly be worth your while to put yourself out of the way for the sake of a few hundred pounds.'

"Now, it is a fact, gentlemen, as you may see for yourselves, that my hair is of a very full and rich tint, so that it seemed to me that, if there was to be any competition in the matter, I stood as good a chance as any man that I had ever met. Vincent Spaulding seemed to know so much about it that I thought he might prove useful, so I just ordered him to put up the shutters for the day and to come right away with me. He was very willing to have a holiday, so we shut the business up and started off for the address that was given us in the advertisement.

"I never hope to see such a sight as that again, Mr. Holmes. From north, south, east, and west every man who had a shade of red in his hair had tramped into the city to answer the advertisement. Every shade of color they were—straw, lemon, orange, brick, Irish setter, liver, clay; but, as Spaulding said, there were not many who had the real vivid flame-colored tint. When I saw how many were waiting, I would have given it up in despair; but Spaulding would not hear of it. How he did it I could not imagine, but he pushed and pulled and butted until he got me through the crowd and right up to the steps which led to the office. There was a double stream upon the stair, some going up in hope, and some coming back dejected; but we wedged in as well as we could and soon found ourselves in the office."

"Your experience has been a most entertaining one," remarked

Holmes, as his client paused and refreshed his memory with a huge pinch of snuff. "Pray continue your very interesting statement."

"There was nothing in the office but a couple of wooden chairs and a deal table, behind which sat a small man, with a head that was even redder than mine. He said a few words to each candidate as he came up, and then he always managed to find some fault in them which would disqualify them. Getting a vacancy did not seem to be such a very easy matter, after all. However, when our turn came, the little man was much more favorable to me than to any of the others, and he closed the door as we entered, so that he might have a private word with us.

"'This is Mr. Jabez Wilson,' said my assistant, 'and he is willing to fill a vacancy in the League.'

"'And he is admirably suited for it,' the other answered. 'He has every requirement. I cannot recall when I have seen anything so fine.' He took a step backward, cocked his head on one side, and gazed at my hair until I felt quite bashful. Then suddenly he plunged forward, wrung my hand, and congratulated me warmly on my success.

"'It would be injustice to hesitate,' said he. 'You will, however, I am sure, excuse me for taking an obvious precaution.' With that he seized my hair in both his hands and tugged until I yelled with pain. 'There is water in your eyes,' said he, as he released me. 'I perceive that all is as it should be. But we have to be careful, for we have twice been deceived by wigs and once by paint.' He stepped over to the window and shouted through it at the top of his voice that the vacancy was filled. A groan of disappointment came up from below, and the folk all trooped away in different directions, until there was not a red head to be seen except my own and that of the manager.

"'My name,' said he, 'is Mr. Duncan Ross, and I am myself one of the pensioners upon the fund left by our noble benefactor. Are you a married man, Mr. Wilson? Have you a family?'

"I answered that I had not.

His face fell immediately.

" 'Dear me!' he said, gravely, 'that is very serious indeed! I am sorry to hear you say that. The fund was, of course, for the propagation and spread of the red-heads as well as for their maintenance. It is exceedingly unfortunate that you should be a bachelor.'

"My face lengthened at this, Mr. Holmes, for I thought that I was not to have the vacancy after all; but, after thinking it over for a few minutes, he said that it would be all right.

" 'In the case of another,' said he, 'the objection might be fatal, but we must stretch a point in favor of a man with such a head of hair as yours. When shall you be able to enter upon your new duties?'

" 'Well, it is a little awkward, for I have a business already,' said I.

" 'Oh, never mind about that, Mr. Wilson!' said Vincent Spaulding. 'I shall be able to look after that for you.'

" 'What would be the hours?' I asked.

" 'Ten to two.'

"Now a pawnbroker's business is mostly done of an evening, Mr. Holmes, especially Thursday and Friday evenings, which is just before payday; so it would suit me very well to earn a little in the mornings. Besides, I knew that my assistant was a good man, and that he would see to anything that turned up.

" 'That would suit me very well,' said I. 'And the pay?'

" 'Is $4 a week.'

" 'And the work?'

" 'Is purely nominal.'

" 'What do you call purely nominal?'

" 'Well, you have to be in the office, or at least in the building, the whole time. If you leave, you forfeit your whole position forever. The will is very clear upon that point. You don't comply with the conditions if you budge from the office during that time.'

" 'It's only four hours a day, and I should not think of leaving,' said I.

" 'No excuse will avail,' said Mr. Duncan Ross, 'neither sickness nor business nor anything else. There you must stay, or you lose your billet.'

" 'And the work?'

" 'Is to copy out the *Encyclopaedia Britannica*. There is the first volume of it in that press. You must find your own ink, pens, and blotting-paper, but we provide this table and chair. Will you be ready tomorrow?'

" 'Certainly,' I answered.

" 'Then, good-bye, Mr. Jabez Wilson, and let me congratulate you once more on the important position which you have been fortunate enough to gain.' He bowed me out of the room, and I went home with my assistant, hardly knowing what to say or do, I was so pleased at my own good fortune.

"Well, I thought over the matter all day, and by evening I was in low spirits again, for I had quite persuaded myself that the whole affair must be some great hoax or fraud, though what its object might be I could not imagine. It seemed altogether past belief that any one could make such a will, or that they would pay such a sum for doing anything so simple as copying out the *Encyclopaedia Britannica*. Vincent Spaulding did what he could to cheer me up, but by bedtime I had reasoned myself out of the whole thing. However, in the morning I determined to have a look at it anyhow, so I bought a penny bottle of ink, and with a quill pen, and seven sheets of foolscap paper, I started off for Pope's Court.

"Well, to my surprise and delight, everything was as right as possible. The table was set out ready for me, and Mr. Duncan Ross was there to see that I got fairly to work. He started me off upon the letter A, and then he left me, but he would drop in from time to time to see that all was right with me. At two o'clock he bade me good day, complimented me upon the amount that I had written, and locked the door of the office after me.

"This went on day after day, Mr. Holmes, and on Saturday the manager came in and planked down four golden sovereigns for my week's work. It was the same next week, and the same the week after. Every morning I was there at ten, and every afternoon I left at two. By degrees Mr. Duncan Ross took to coming in only once of a morning, and then, after a time, he did not come in at all. Still, of course, I never dared to leave the room for an instant, for I was not sure when he might come, and the billet was such a good one, and suited me so well, that I would not risk the loss of it.

"Eight weeks passed away like this, and I had written about Abbots and Archery and Armor and Architecture and Attica, and hoped with diligence that I might get on to the B's before very long. It cost me something in foolscap, and I had pretty nearly filled a shelf with my writings. And then suddenly the whole business came to an end."

"To an end?"

"Yes, sir. And no later than this morning. I went to my work as usual at ten o'clock, but the door was shut and locked, with a little square of cardboard hammered onto the middle of the panel with a tack. Here it is, and you can read for yourself."

He held up a piece of white cardboard about the size of a sheet of notepaper. It read in this fashion:

THE RED-HEADED LEAGUE
IS
DISSOLVED.
October 9, 1890.

Sherlock Holmes and I surveyed this curt announcement and the rueful face behind it, until the comical side of the affair so completely overtopped every other consideration that we both burst out into a roar of laughter.

"I cannot see that there is anything very funny," cried our client, flushing up to the roots of his flaming head. "If you can do nothing better than laugh at me, I can go elsewhere."

"No, no," cried Holmes, shoving him back into the chair from which he had half risen. "I really wouldn't miss your case for the world. It is most refreshingly unusual. But there is, if you will excuse my saying so, something just a little funny about it. Pray what steps did you take when you found the card upon the door?"

"I was staggered, sir. I did not know what to do. Then I called round at the office, but none of them seemed to know anything about it. Finally, I went to the landlord, who is an accountant living on the ground floor, and I asked him if he could tell me what had become of the Red-headed League. He said that he had never heard of any such body. Then I asked him who Mr. Duncan Ross was. He answered that the name was new to him.

" 'Well,' said I, 'the gentleman at No. 4.'

" 'What, the red-headed man?'

" 'Yes.'

" 'Oh,' said he, 'his name was William Morris. He was a solicitor and was using my room as a temporary convenience until his new premises were ready. He moved out yesterday.'

" 'Where could I find him?'

" 'Oh, at his new offices. He did tell me the address. Yes, 17 King Edward Street, near St. Paul's.'

"I started off, Mr. Holmes, but when I got to that address it was a manufactory of artificial kneecaps, and no one in it had ever heard of either Mr. William Morris or Mr. Duncan Ross."

"And what did you do then?" asked Holmes.

"I went home to Saxe-Coburg Square, and I took the advice of my assistant. But he could not help me in any way. He could only say that if I waited I should hear by post. But that was not quite good enough, Mr. Holmes. I did not wish to lose such a place without a struggle, so, as I had heard that you were good enough to give advice to poor folk who were in need of it, I came right away to you."

"And you did very wisely," said Holmes. "Your case is an exceedingly remarkable one, and I shall be happy to look into it. From what you have told me I think that it is possible that graver issues hang from it than might at first sight appear."

"Grave enough!" said Mr. Jabez Wilson. "Why, I have lost four pounds a week."

"As far as you are personally concerned," remarked Holmes, "I do not see that you have any grievance against this extraordinary league. On the contrary, you are, as I understand, richer by some

£30, to say nothing of the minute knowledge which you have gained on every subject which comes under the letter A. You have lost nothing by them."

"No, sir. But I want to find out about them, and who they are, and what their object was in playing this prank—if it was a prank —upon me. It was a pretty expensive joke for them, for it cost them two and thirty pounds."

"We shall endeavor to clear up these points for you. And, first, one or two questions, Mr. Wilson. This assistant of yours who first called your attention to the advertisement—how long had he been with you?"

"About a month then."

"How did he come?"

"In answer to an advertisement."

"Was he the only applicant?"

"No, I had a dozen."

"Why did you pick him?"

"Because he was handy and would come cheap."

"At half-wages, in fact."

"Yes."

"What is he like, this Vincent Spaulding?"

"Small, stout-built, very quick in his ways, no hair on his face, though he's not short of thirty. Has a white splash of acid upon his forehead."

Holmes sat up in his chair in considerable excitement. "I thought as much," said he. "Have you ever observed that his ears are pierced for earrings?"

"Yes, sir. He told me that a gypsy had done it for him when he was a lad."

"Hum!" said Holmes, sinking back in deep thought. "He is still with you?"

"Oh yes, sir; I have only just left him."

"And has your business been attended to in your absence?"

"Nothing to complain of, sir. There's never very much to do of a morning."

"That will do, Mr. Wilson. I shall be happy to give you an opinion upon the subject in the course of a day or two. Today is Saturday, and I hope that by Monday we may come to a conclusion."

"Well, Watson," said Holmes, when our visitor had left us, "what do you make of it all?"

"I make nothing of it," I answered, frankly. "It is a most mysterious business."

"As a rule," said Holmes, "the more bizarre a thing is the less mysterious it proves to be. It is your commonplace, featureless crimes which are really puzzling, just as a commonplace face is the most difficult to identify. But I must be prompt over this matter."

"What are you going to do, then?" I asked.

"To smoke," he answered. "It is quite a three-pipe problem, and I beg that you won't speak to me for fifty minutes." He curled himself up in his chair, with his thin knees drawn up to his hawk-like nose, and there he sat with his eyes closed and his black clay pipe thrusting out like the bill of some strange bird. I had come to the conclusion that he had dropped asleep, and indeed was nodding myself, when he suddenly sprang out of his chair with the gesture of a man who has made up his mind, and put his pipe down upon the mantelpiece.

"Sarasate plays at the St. James's Hall this afternoon," he remarked. "What do you think, Watson? Could your patients spare you for a few hours?"

"I have nothing to do today. My practice is never very absorbing."

"Then put on your hat and come. I am going through the city first, and we can have some lunch on the way. I observe that there is a good deal of German music on the program, which is rather more to my taste than Italian or French. It is introspective, and I want to introspect. Come along!"

We traveled by the Underground as far as Aldersgate; and a short walk took us to Saxe-Coburg Square, the scene of the singular story which we had listened to in the morning. It was a pokey, little, shabby-genteel place, where four lines of dingy two-storied brick houses looked out into a small railed-in enclosure, where a lawn of weedy grass and a few clumps of faded laurel bushes made a hard fight against a smoke laden and uncongenial atmosphere. Three gilt balls and a brown board with *"Jabez Wilson"* in white letters, upon a corner house, announced the place where our red-headed client carried on his business. Sherlock Holmes stopped in front of it with his head on one side, and looked it all over, with his eyes shining brightly between puckered lids. Then he walked slowly up the street, and then down again to the corner, still looking keenly at the houses. Finally he returned to the pawnbroker's, and, having thumped vigorously upon the pavement with his stick two or three times, he went up to the door and knocked. It was instantly opened by a bright-looking, clean-shaven young fellow, who asked him to step in.

"Thank you," said Holmes. "I only wished to ask you how you would go from here to the Strand."

"Third right, fourth left," answered the assistant, promptly, closing the door.

"Smart fellow, that," observed Holmes, as we walked away. "He is, in my judgment, the fourth smartest man in London, and for daring I am not sure that he has not a claim to be third. I have known something of him before."

"Evidently," said I, "Mr. Wilson's assistant counts for a good deal in this mystery of the Red-headed League. I am sure that you inquired your way merely in order that you might see him."

"Not him."

"What then?"

"The knees of his trousers."

"And what did you see?"

"What I expected to see."

"Why did you beat the pavement?"

"My dear doctor, this is a time for observation, not for talk. We are spies in an enemy's country. We know something of Saxe-Coburg Square. Let us now explore the parts which lie behind it."

The road in which we found ourselves as we turned round the corner from the retired Saxe-Coburg Square presented as great a contrast to it as the front of a picture does to the back. It was one of the main arteries which convey the traffic of the city to the north and west. The roadway was blocked with the immense stream of commerce flowing in a double tide inward and outward, while the footpaths were black with the hurrying swarm of pedestrians. It was difficult to realize as we looked at the line of fine shops and stately business premises that they really abutted on the other side upon the faded and stagnant square which we had just quitted.

"Let me see," said Holmes, standing at the corner, and glancing along the line, "I should like just to remember the order of the houses here. It is a hobby of mine to have an exact knowledge of London. There is Mortimer's, the tobacconist, the little newspaper shop, the Coburg branch of the City and Suburban Bank, the Vegetarian Restaurant, and McFarlane's carriage-building depot. That carries us right on to the other block. And now, doctor, we've done our work, so it's time we had some play. A sandwich and a cup of coffee, and then off to violin-land, where all is sweetness and delicacy and harmony, and there are no red-headed clients to vex us with their conundrums."

My friend was an enthusiastic musician, being himself not only a very capable performer, but a composer of no ordinary merit. All the afternoon he sat in the stalls wrapped in the most perfect happiness, gently waving his long, thin fingers in time to the music, while his gently smiling face and his languid, dreamy eyes were as unlike those of Holmes, the sleuthhound, Holmes the relentless, keen-witted, ready-handed criminal agent, as it was possible to conceive.

"You want to go home, no doubt, doctor," he remarked, as we emerged.

"Yes, it would be as well."

"And I have some business to do which will take some hours. This business at Coburg Square is serious."

"Why serious?"

"A considerable crime is in contemplation. I have every reason to believe that we shall be in time to stop it. But today being Saturday rather complicates matters. I shall want your help tonight."

"At what time?"

"Ten will be early enough."

"I shall be at Baker Street at ten."

"Very well. And, I say, doctor, there may be some little danger, so kindly put your army revolver in your pocket." He waved his hand, turned on his heel, and disappeared in an instant among the crowd.

I trust that I am not more dense than my neighbors, but I was always oppressed with a sense of my own stupidity in my dealings with Sherlock Holmes. Here I had heard what he had heard, I had seen what he had seen, and yet from his words it was evident that he saw clearly not only what had happened, but what was about to happen, while to me the whole business was still confused and grotesque. As I drove home to my house in Kensington I thought over it all, from the extraordinary story of the red-headed copier of the *Encyclopaedia* down to the visit to Saxe-Coburg Square, and the ominous words with which he had parted from me. What was this nocturnal expedition, and why should I go armed? Where were we going, and what were we to do? I had the hint from Holmes that this smooth-faced pawnbroker's assistant was a form-idable man—a man who might play a deep game. I tried to puzzle it out, but gave it up in despair and set the matter aside until night should bring an explanation.

It was a quarter-past nine when I started from home and made my way across the Park, and so through Oxford Street to Baker Street. Two hansoms were standing at the door, and, as I entered the passage, I heard the sound of voices from above. On entering his room I found Holmes in animated conversation with two men, one of whom I recognized as Peter Jones, the official police agent, while the other was a long, thin, sad-faced man, with a very shiny hat and oppressively respectable frock coat.

"Ha! our party is complete," said Holmes, buttoning up his pea jacket and taking his heavy hunting crop from the rack. "Watson, I think you know Mr. Jones, of Scotland Yard? Let me introduce you to Mr. Merryweather, who is to be our companion in tonight's adventure."

"We're hunting in couples again, doctor, you see," said Jones, in his consequential way. "Our friend here is a wonderful man for starting a chase. All he wants is an old dog to help him to do the running down."

"I hope a wild goose may not prove to be the end of our chase," observed Mr. Merryweather, gloomily.

"You may place considerable confidence in Mr. Holmes, sir,"

said the police agent, loftily. "He has his own little methods, which are, if he won't mind my saying so, just a little too theoretical and fantastic, but he has the makings of a detective in him. It is not too much to say that once or twice, as in that business of the Sholto murder and the Agra treasure, he has been more nearly correct than the official force."

"Oh, if you say so, Mr. Jones, it is all right," said the stranger, with deference. "Still, I confess that I miss my rubber. It is the first Saturday night for seven-and-twenty years that I have not had my rubber."

"I think you will find," said Sherlock Holmes, "that you will play for a higher stake tonight than you have ever done yet, and that the play will be more exciting. For you, Mr. Merryweather, the stake will be some £30,000; and for you, Jones, it will be the man upon whom you wish to lay your hands."

"John Clay, the murderer, thief, smasher, and forger. He's a young man, Mr. Merryweather, but he is at the head of his profession, and I would rather have my bracelets on him than on any criminal in London. He's a remarkable man, is young John Clay. His grandfather was a royal duke, and he himself has been to Eton and Oxford. His brain is as cunning as his fingers, and though we meet signs of him at every turn, we never know where to find the man himself. He'll crack a crib in Scotland one week and be raising money to build an orphanage in Cornwall the next. I've been on his track for years and have never set eyes on him yet."

"I hope that I may have the pleasure of introducing you tonight. I've had one or two little turns also with Mr. John Clay, and I agree with you that he is at the head of his profession. It is past ten, however, and quite time that we started. If you two will take the first hansom, Watson and I will follow in the second."

Sherlock Holmes was not very communicative during the long drive and lay back in the cab humming the tunes which he had heard in the afternoon. We rattled through a labyrinth of gas-lit streets until we emerged into Farrington Street.

"We are close there now," my friend remarked. "This fellow

Merryweather is a bank director and personally interested in the matter. I thought it as well to have Jones with us also. He is not a bad fellow, though an absolute imbecile in his profession. He has one positive virtue. He is as brave as a bulldog and as tenacious as a lobster if he gets his claws upon any one. Here we are, and they are waiting for us."

We had reached the same crowded thoroughfare in which we had found ourselves in the morning. Our cabs were dismissed, and, following the guidance of Mr. Merryweather, we passed down a narrow passage and through a side door, which he opened for us. Within there was a small corridor, which ended in a very massive iron gate. This also was opened, and led down a flight of winding stone steps, which terminated at another formidable gate. Mr. Merryweather stopped to light a lantern and then conducted us down a dark, earth-smelling passage, and so, after opening a third door, into a huge vault or cellar, which was piled all round with crates and massive boxes.

"You are not very vulnerable from above," Holmes remarked, as he held up the lantern and gazed about him.

"Nor from below," said Mr. Merryweather, striking his stick upon the flags which lined the floor. "Why, dear me, it sounds quite hollow!" he remarked, looking up in surprise.

"I must really ask you to be a little more quiet," said Holmes, severely. "You have already imperiled the whole success of our expedition. Might I beg that you would have the goodness to sit down upon one of those boxes and not to interfere?"

The solemn Mr. Merryweather perched himself upon a crate, with a very injured expression upon his face, while Holmes fell upon his knees upon the floor, and, with the lantern and a magnifying lens, began to examine minutely the cracks between the stones. A few seconds sufficed to satisfy him, for he sprang to his feet again and put his glass in his pocket.

"We have at least an hour before us," he remarked; "for they can hardly take any steps until the good pawnbroker is safely in bed. Then they will not lose a minute, for the sooner they do their work the longer time they will have for their escape. We are at present, doctor—as no doubt you have divined—in the cellar of the city branch of one of the principal London banks. Mr. Merryweather is the chairman of directors, and he will explain to you that there are reasons why the more daring criminals of London should take a considerable interest in this cellar at present."

"It is our French gold," whispered the director. "We have had several warnings that an attempt might be made upon it."

"Your French gold?"

"Yes. We had occasion some months ago to strengthen our resources, and borrowed, for that purpose, 30,000 napoleons from the Bank of France. It has become known that we have never had occasion to unpack the money, and that it is still lying in our cellar. The crate upon which I sit contains 2000 napoleons packed between layers of lead foil. Our reserve of bullion is much larger at present than is usually kept in a single branch office, and the directors have had misgivings upon the subject."

"Which were very well justified," observed Holmes. "And now it is time that we arranged our little plans. I expect that within an hour matters will come to a head. In the meantime, Mr. Merryweather, we must put the screen over that dark lantern."

"And sit in the dark?"

"I am afraid so. I had brought a pack of cards in my pocket, and I thought that you might have your rubber after all. But I see that the enemy's preparations have gone so far that we cannot risk the presence of a light. And, first of all, we must choose our positions. These are daring men, and though we shall take them at a disadvantage, they may do us some harm unless we are careful. I shall stand behind this crate, and you conceal yourselves behind those. Then, when I flash a light upon them, close in swiftly. If they fire, Watson, have no compunction about shooting them down."

I placed my revolver, cocked, upon the top of the wooden case behind which I crouched. Holmes shot the slide across the front of his lantern, and left us in pitch darkness—such an absolute darkness as I have never before experienced. The smell of hot metal remained to assure us that the light was still there, ready to flash out at a moment's notice. To me, with my nerves worked up to a pitch of expectancy, there was something depressing and subduing in the sudden gloom, and in the cold, dank air of the vault.

"They have but one retreat," whispered Holmes. "That is back through the house into Saxe-Coburg Square. I hope that you have done what I asked you, Jones?"

"I have an inspector and two officers waiting at the front door."

"Then we have stopped all the holes. And now we must be silent and wait."

What a time it seemed! From comparing notes afterwards it was but an hour and a quarter, yet it appeared to me that the night must have almost gone, and the dawn be breaking above us. My limbs were weary and stiff, for I feared to change my position; yet my nerves were worked up to the highest pitch of tension, and my hearing was so acute that I could not only hear the gentle breathing of my companions, but I could distinguish the deeper, heavier in-breath of the bulky Jones from the thin, sighing note of the bank director. From my position I could look over the case in the direction of the floor. Suddenly my eyes caught the glint of a light.

At first it was but a lurid spark upon the stone pavement. Then it lengthened out until it became a yellow line, and then, without any warning or sound, a gash seemed to open and a hand appeared, a white, almost womanly hand, which felt about in the center of the little area of light. For a minute or more the hand, with its writhing fingers, protruded out of the floor. Then it was withdrawn as suddenly as it appeared, and all was dark again save the single lurid spark which marked a chink between the stones.

Its disappearance, however, was but momentary. With a rending, tearing sound, one of the broad, white stones turned over upon its side and left a square, gaping hole, through which streamed the light of a lantern. Over the edge there peeped a clean-cut, boyish face, which looked keenly about it, and then, with a hand on either side of the aperture, drew itself shoulder-high and waist-high, until one knee rested upon the edge. In another instant he stood at the side of the hole, and was hauling after him a companion,

lithe and small like himself, with a pale face and a shock of very red hair.

"It's all clear," he whispered. "Have you the chisel and the bags. Great Scott! Jump, Archie, jump, and I'll swing for it!"

Sherlock Holmes had sprung out and seized the intruder by the collar. The other dived down the hole, and I heard the sound of rending cloth as Jones clutched at his skirts. The light flashed upon the barrel of a revolver, but Holmes's hunting crop came down on the man's wrist, and the pistol clinked upon the stone floor.

"It's no use, John Clay," said Holmes, blandly. "You have no chance at all."

"So I see," the other answered, with the utmost coolness. "I fancy that my pal is all right, though I see you have got his coat-tails."

"There are three men waiting for him at the door."

"Oh, indeed! You seem to have done the thing very completely. I must compliment you."

"And I you," Holmes answered. "Your red-headed idea was very new and effective."

"You'll see your pal again presently," said Jones. "He's quicker at climbing down holes than I am. Just hold out while I fix the derbies."

"I beg that you will not touch me with your filthy hands," remarked our prisoner, as the handcuffs clattered upon his wrists. "You may not be aware that I have royal blood in my viens. Have the goodness, also, when you address me always to say 'sir' and 'please.'"

"All right," said Jones, with a stare and a snigger. "Well, would you please, sir, march upstairs, where we can get a cab to carry your highness to the police station?"

"That is better," said John Clay, serenely. He made a sweeping bow to the three of us and walked quietly off in the custody of the detective.

"Really, Mr. Holmes," said Mr. Merryweather, as we followed them from the cellar, "I do not know how the bank can thank you or repay you. There is no doubt that you have detected and defeated in the most complete manner one of the most determined attempts at bank robbery that have ever come within my experience."

"I have had one or two little scores of my own to settle with Mr. John Clay," said Holmes. "I have been at some small expense over this matter, which I shall expect the bank to refund, but beyond that I am amply repaid by having had an experience which is in many ways unique, and by hearing the very remarkable narrative of the Red-headed League."

"You see, Watson," he explained, in the early hours of the morning, when we were back in Baker Street, "it was perfectly obvious from the first that the only possible object of this rather fantastic business of the advertisement of the League, and the copying of the *Encyclopaedia,* must be to get this not over-bright pawnbroker out of the way for a number of hours every day. It was a curious way of managing it, but, really, it would be difficult to suggest a better. The method was no doubt suggested to Clay's ingenious mind by the color of his accomplice's hair. The £4 a week was a lure which must draw him, and what was it to them, who were playing for thousands? They put in the advertisement, one rogue has the temporary office, the other rogue incites the man to apply for it, and together they manage to secure his absence every morning in the week. From the time that I heard of the assistant having come for half-wages, it was obvious to me that he had some strong motive for securing the situation."

"But how could you guess what the motive was?"

"The man's business was a small one, and there was nothing in his house which could account for such elaborate preparations, and such an expenditure as they were at. It must, then, be something out of the house. What could it be? I thought of the assistant's fondness for photography, and his trick of vanishing into the cellar. The cellar! There was the end of this tangled clue. Then I made inquiries as to this mysterious assistant and found that I had to deal with one of the coolest and most daring criminals in London. He was doing something in the cellar—something which took many hours a day for months on end. What could it be, once more? I could think of nothing save that he was running a tunnel to some other building.

"So far I had got when we went to visit the scene of action. I surprised you by beating upon the pavement with my stick. I was ascertaining whether the cellar stretched out in front or behind. It was not in front. Then I rang the bell, and, as I hoped, the assistant answered it. We have had some skirmishes, but we had never set eyes upon each other before. I hardly looked at his face. His knees were what I wished to see. You must yourself have remarked how worn, wrinkled, and stained they were. They spoke of those hours of burrowing. The only remaining point was what they were burrowing for. I walked round the corner, saw that the City and Suburban Bank abutted on our friend's premises, and felt that I had solved my problem. When you drove home after the concert I called upon Scotland Yard and upon the chairman of the bank directors, with the result that you have seen."

"And how could you tell that they would make their attempt tonight?" I asked.

"Well, when they closed their League offices that was a sign that they cared no longer about Mr. Jabez Wilson's presence—in other words, that they had completed their tunnel. But it was essential that they should use it soon, as it might be discovered, or the bullion might be removed. Saturday would suit them better than any other day, as it would give them two days for their escape. For all these reasons I expected them to come tonight."

"You reasoned it out beautifully," I exclaimed, in unfeigned admiration. "It is so long a chain, and yet every link rings true."

"It saved me from ennui," he answered, yawning. "Alas! I already feel it closing in upon me. My life is spent in one long effort to escape from the commonplaces of existence. These little problems help me to do so."

"And you are a benefactor of the race," said I.

He shrugged his shoulders. "Well, perhaps, after all, it is of some little use," he remarked. " '*L'homme c'est rien—l'oeuvre c'est tout,*' as Gustave Flaubert wrote to Georges Sand."

THE TREASURE IN THE CAVE

From *The Adventures of Tom Sawyer*

MARK TWAIN

There comes a time in every rightly constructed boy's life when he has a raging desire to go somewhere and dig for hidden treasure. This desire suddenly came upon Tom one day. He sallied out to find Joe Harper, but failed of success. Next he sought Ben Rogers; he had gone fishing. Presently he stumbled upon Huck Finn the Red-Handed. Huck would answer. Tom took him to a private place and opened the matter to him confidentially. Huck was willing. Huck was always willing to take a hand in any enterprise that offered entertainment and required no capital, for he had a troublesome superabundance of that sort of time which is *not* money. "Where'll we dig?" said Huck.

"Oh, most anywhere."

"Why, is it hid all around?"

"No indeed it ain't. It's hid in mighty particular places, Huck—sometimes on islands, sometimes in rotten chests under the end of a limb of an old dead tree, just where the shadow falls at midnight; but mostly under the floor in ha'nted houses."

"Who hides it?"

"Why, robbers, of course—who'd you reckon? Sunday school sup'rintendents?"

"I don't know. If 'twas mine I wouldn't hide it; I'd spend it and have a good time."

"So would I. But robbers don't do that way. They always hide it and leave it there."

"Don't they come after it any more?"

"No, they think they will, but they generally forget the marks, or else they die. Anyway, it lays there a long time and gets rusty; and by and by somebody finds an old yellow paper that tells how to find the marks—a paper that's got to be ciphered over about a week because it's mostly signs and hy'roglyphics."

"Hyro—which?"

"Hy'roglyphics—pictures and things, you know, that don't seem to mean anything."

"Have you got one of them papers, Tom?"

"No."

"Well then, how you going to find the marks?"

"I don't want any marks. They always bury it under a ha'nted house or on an island, or under a dead tree that's got one limb sticking out. Well, we've tried Jackson's Island a little, and we can try it again some time; and there's the old ha'nted house up the Still-House branch, and there's lots of dead-limb trees—dead loads of 'em."

"Is it under all of them?"

"How you talk! No!"

"Then how you going to know which one to go for?"

"Go for all of 'em!"

"Why, Tom, it 'll take all summer."

"Well, what of that? Suppose you find a brass pot with a hundred dollars in it, all rusty and gray, or a rotten chest full of di'monds. How's that?"

Huck's eyes glowed.

"That's bully. Plenty bully enough for me. Just you gimme the hundred dollars and I don't want no di'monds."

"All right. But I bet you *I* ain't going to throw off on di'monds. Some of 'em's worth twenty dollars apiece—there ain't any, hardly, but's worth six bits or a dollar." ·

"No? Is that so?"

"Cert'nly—anybody 'll tell you so. Hain't you ever seen one, Huck?"

"Not as I remember."

"Oh, kings have slathers of them."

"Well, I don't know no kings, Tom. But say—where you going to dig first?"

"Well, I don't know. S'pose we tackle that old dead-limb tree on the hill t'other side of Still-House branch?"

"I'm agreed."

So they got a crippled pick and a shovel, and set out on their three-mile tramp. They arrived hot and panting, and threw themselves down in the shade of a neighboring elm to rest and have a smoke.

"I like this," said Tom.

"So do I."

"Say, Huck, if we find a treasure here, what you going to do with your share?"

"Well, I'll have pie and a glass of soda every day, and I'll go to every circus that comes along. I bet I'll have a gay time."

"Well, ain't you going to save any of it?"

"Save it? What for?"

"Why, so as to have something to live on, by and by."

"Oh, that ain't any use. Pap would come back to thish yer town some day and get his claws on it if I didn't hurry up, and I tell you he'd clean it out pretty quick. What you going to do with yourn, Tom?"

"I'm going to buy a new drum, and sure-'nough sword, and a red necktie and a bull pup, and get married."

"Married!"

"That's it."

"Tom, you—why, you ain't in your right mind."

"Wait—you'll see."

"Well, that's the foolishest thing you could do. Look at pap and my mother. Fight! Why, they used to fight all the time. I remember, mighty well."

"That ain't anything. The girl I'm going to marry won't fight."

"Tom, I reckon they're all alike. They'll all comb a body. Now you better think 'bout this awhile. I tell you you better. What's the name of the gal?"

"It ain't a gal at all—it's a girl."

"It's all the same, I reckon; some says gal, some says girl—both's right, like enough. Anyway, what's her name, Tom?"

"I'll tell you some time—not now."

"All right—that 'll do. Only if you get married I'll be more lonesomer than ever."

"No you won't. You'll come and live with me. Now stir out of this and we'll go to digging."

They worked and sweated for half an hour. No result. They toiled another half-hour. Still no result. Huck said:

"Do they always bury it as deep as this?"

"Sometimes—not always. Not generally. I reckon we haven't got the right place."

So they chose a new spot and began again. The labor dragged a little, but still they made progress. They pegged away in silence for some time. Finally Huck leaned on his shovel, swabbed the beaded drops from his brow with his sleeve, and said:

"Where you going to dig next, after we get this one?"

"I reckon maybe we'll tackle the old tree that's over yonder on

Cardiff Hill back of the widow's."

"I reckon that 'll be a good one. But won't the widow take it away from us, Tom? It's on her land."

"*She* take it away! Maybe she'd like to try it once. Whoever finds one of these hid treasures, it belongs to him. It don't make any difference whose land it's on."

That was satisfactory. The work went on. By and by Huck said:

"Blame it, we must be in the wrong place again. What do you think?"

"It *is* mighty curious, Huck. I don't understand it. Sometimes witches interfere. I reckon maybe that's what's the trouble now."

"Shucks, witches ain't got no power in the daytime."

"Well, that's so. I didn't think of that. Oh, *I* know what the matter is! What a blamed lot of fools we are! You got to find out where the shadow of the limb falls at midnight, and that's where you dig!"

"Then consound it, we've fooled away all this work for nothing. Now hang it all, we got to come back in the night. It's an awful long way. Can you get out?"

"I bet I will. We've got to do it to-night, too, because if somebody sees these holes they'll know in a minute what's here and they'll go for it."

"Well, I'll come around and maow to-night."

"All right. Let's hide the tools in the bushes."

The boys were there that night, about the appointed time. They sat in the shadow waiting. It was a lonely place, and an hour made solemn by old traditions. Spirits whispered in the rustling leaves, ghosts lurked in the murky nooks, the deep baying of a hound floated up out of the distance, an owl answered with his sepulchral note. The boys were subdued by these solemnities, and talked little. By and by they judged that twelve had come; they marked where the shadow fell, and began to dig. Their hopes commenced to rise. Their interest grew stronger, and their industry kept pace with it. The hole deepened and still deepened, but

every time their hearts jumped to hear the pick strike upon something, they only suffered a new disappointment. It was only a stone
or a chunk. At last Tom said:

"It ain't any use, Huck, we're wrong again."

"Well, but we *can't* be wrong. We spotted the shadder to a dot."

"I know it, but then there's another thing."

"What's that?"

"Why, we only guessed at the time. Like enough it was too late
or too early."

Huck dropped his shovel.

"That's it," said he. "That's the very trouble. We got to give this
one up. We can't ever tell the right time, and besides this kind of
thing's too awful, here this time of night with witches and ghosts
a-fluttering around so. I feel as if something's behind me all the
time; and I'm afeard to turn around, becuz maybe there's others
in front a-waiting for a chance. I been creeping all over, ever since
I got here."

"Well, I've been pretty much so, too, Huck. They most always
put in a dead man when they bury a treasure under a tree, to look
out for it."

"Lordy!"

"Yes, they do. I've always heard that."

"Tom, I don't like to fool around much where there's dead
people. A body's bound to get into trouble with 'em, sure."

"I don't like to stir 'em up, either. S'pose this one here was to
stick his skull out and say something!"

"Don't, Tom! It's awful."

"Well, it just is. Huck, I don't feel comfortable a bit."

"Say, Tom, let's give this place up, and try somewheres else."

"All right, I reckon we better."

"What'll it be?"

Tom considered awhile, and then said:

"The ha'nted house. That's it!"

"Blame it, I don't like ha'nted houses, Tom. Why, there's a dern
sight worse'n dead people. Dead people might talk, maybe, but

they don't come sliding around in a shroud, when you ain't noticing, and peep over your shoulder all of a sudden and grit their teeth, the way a ghost does. I couldn't stand such a thing as that, Tom—nobody could."

"Yes, but, Huck, ghosts don't travel around only at night. They won't hender us from digging there in the daytime."

"Well, all right. We'll tackle the ha'nted house if you say so—but I reckon it's taking chances."

They had started down the hill by this time. There in the middle of the moonlit valley below them stood the "ha'nted" house, utterly isolated, its fences gone long ago, rank weeds smothering the very doorsteps, the chimney crumbled to ruin, the window-sashes vacant, a corner of the roof caved in. The boys gazed awhile; then talking in a low tone, as befitted the time and the circumstances, they struck far off to the right, to give the haunted house a wide berth, and took their way homeward through the woods that adorned the rearward side of Cardiff Hill.

About noon the next day the boys arrived at the dead tree; they had come for their tools. Tom was impatient to go to the haunted house; Huck was measurably so, also—but suddenly said:

"Lookyhere, Tom, do you know what day it is?"

Tom mentally ran over the days of the week, and then quickly lifted his eyes with a startled look in them—

"My! I never once thought of it, Huck!"

"Well, I didn't neither, but all at once it popped onto me that it was Friday."

"Blame it, a body can't be too careful, Huck. We might 'a' got into an awful scrape, tackling such a thing on a Friday."

"*Might!* Better say we *would!* There's some lucky days, maybe, but Friday ain't."

"Any fool knows that. I don't reckon *you* was the first that found it out, Huck."

"Well, I never said I was, did I? And Friday ain't all, neither. I had a rotten bad dream last night—dreampt about rats."

"No! Sure sign of trouble. Did they fight?"

"No."

"Well, that's good, Huck. When they don't fight it's only a sign that there's trouble around, you know. All we got to do is to look mighty sharp and keep out of it. We'll drop this thing for to-day, and play. Do you know Robin Hood, Huck?"

"No. Who's Robin Hood?"

"Why, he was one of the greatest men that was ever in England —and the best. He was a robber."

"Cracky, I wisht I was. Who did he rob?"

"Only sheriffs and bishops and rich people and kings, and such like. But he never bothered the poor. He loved 'em. He always divided up with 'em perfectly square."

"Well, he must 'a' been a brick."

"I bet you he was, Huck. Oh, he was the noblest man that ever was. They ain't any such men now, I can tell you. He could lick any man in England, with one hand tied behind him; and he could take his yew bow and plug a ten-cent piece every time, a mile and a half."

"What's a *yew* bow?"

"*I* don't know. It's some kind of a bow, of course. And if he hit that dime only on the edge he would set down and cry—and curse. But we'll play Robin Hood—it's nobby fun. I'll learn you."

"I'm agreed."

So they played Robin Hood all the afternoon, now and then casting a yearning eye down upon the haunted house and passing a remark about the morrow's prospects and possibilities there. As the sun began to sink into the west they took their way homeward athwart the long shadows of the trees and soon were buried from sight in the forests of Cardiff Hill.

On Saturday, shortly after noon, the boys were at the dead tree again. They had a smoke and a chat in the shade, and then dug a little in their last hole, not with great hope, but merely because Tom said there were so many cases where people had given up a treasure after getting down within six inches of it, and then somebody else had come along and turned it up with a single thrust of a shovel. The thing failed this time, however, so the boys shouldered their tools and went away feeling that they had not trifled with fortune, but had fulfilled all the requirements that belong to the business of treasure-hunting.

When they reached the haunted house there was something so weird and grisly about the dead silence that reigned there under the baking sun, and something so depressing about the loneliness and desolation of the place, that they were afraid, for a moment, to venture in. Then they crept to the door and took a trembling peep. They saw a weed-grown, floorless room, unplastered, an ancient fireplace, vacant windows, a ruinous staircase; and here, there and everywhere hung ragged and abandoned cobwebs. They presently entered, softly, with quickened pulses, talking in whispers, ears alert to catch the slightest sound, and muscles tense and ready for instant retreat.

In a little while familiarity modified their fears and they gave the place a critical and interested examination, rather admiring their own boldness, and wondering at it, too. Next they wanted to look up-stairs. This was something like cutting off retreat, but they got to daring each other, and of course there could be but one result—they threw their tools into a corner and made the ascent. Up there were the same signs of decay. In one corner they found a closet that promised mystery, but the promise was a fraud—there was nothing in it. Their courage was up now and well in hand. They were about to go down and begin work when—

"'Sh!" said Tom.

"What is it?" whispered Huck, blanching with fright.

"'Sh! . . . There! . . . Hear it?"

"Yes! . . . Oh, my! Let's run!"

"Keep still! Don't you budge! They're coming right toward the door."

The boys stretched themselves upon the floor with their eyes to knot-holes in the planking, and lay waiting, in a misery of fear.

"They've stopped. . . . No—coming. . . . Here they are. Don't whisper another word, Huck. My goodness, I wish I was out of this!"

Two men entered. Each boy said to himself: "There's the old deaf and dumb Spaniard that's been about town once or twice lately—never saw t'other man before."

"T'other" was a ragged, unkempt creature, with nothing very pleasant in his face. The Spaniard was wrapped in a *serape;* he had bushy white whiskers; long white hair flowed from under his sombrero, and he wore green goggles. When they came in, "t'other" was talking in a low voice; they sat down on the ground, facing the door, with their backs to the wall, and the speaker continued his remarks. His manner became less guarded and his words more distinct as he proceeded:

"No," said he, "I've thought it all over, and I don't like it. It's dangerous."

"Dangerous!" grunted the "deaf and dumb" Spaniard—to the vast surprise of the boys. "Milksop!"

This voice made the boys gasp and quake. It was Injun Joe's!

The two men got out some food and made a luncheon. After a long and thoughtful silence, Injun Joe said:

"Look here, lad—you go back up the river where you belong. Wait there till you hear from me. I'll take the chances on dropping into this town just once more, for a look. We'll do that 'dangerous' job after I've spied around a little and think things look well for it. Then for Texas! We'll leg it together!"

This was satisfactory. Both men presently fell to yawning, and Injun Joe said:

"I'm dead for sleep! It's your turn to watch."

He curled down in the weeds and soon began to snore. His comrade stirred him once or twice and he became quiet. Presently the watcher began to nod; his head drooped lower and lower, both men began to snore now.

The boys drew a long, grateful breath. Tom whispered:

"Now's our chance—come!"

Huck said:

"I can't—I'd die if they was to wake."

Tom urged—Huck held back. At last Tom rose slowly and softly, and started alone. But the first step he made wrung such a hideous creak from the crazy floor that he sank down almost dead with fright. He never made a second attempt. The boys lay there counting the dragging moments till it seemed to them that time must be done and eternity growing gray; and then they were grateful to note that at last the sun was setting.

Now one snore ceased. Injun Joe sat up, stared around—smiled grimly upon his comrade, whose head was drooping upon his knees—stirred him up with his foot and said:

"Here! *You're* a watchman, ain't you! All right, though—nothing's happened."

"My! have I been asleep?"

"Oh, partly, partly. Nearly time for us to be moving, pard. What'll we do with what little swag we've got left?"

"I don't know—leave it here as we've always done, I reckon. No use to take it away till we start south. Six hundred and fifty in silver's something to carry."

"Well—all right—it won't matter to come here once more."

"No—but I'd say come in the night as we used to do—it's better."

"Yes: but look here; it may be a good while before I get the right chance at that job; accidents might happen; 'tain't in such a very good place; we'll just regularly bury it—and bury it deep."

"Good idea," said the comrade, who walked across the room, knelt down, raised one of the rearward hearthstones and took out a bag that jingled pleasantly. He subtracted from it twenty or thirty dollars for himself and as much for Injun Joe and passed the bag to the latter, who was on his knees in the corner, now, digging with his bowie-knife.

The boys forgot all their fears, all their miseries in an instant. With gloating eyes they watched every movement. Luck!—the splendor of it was beyond all imagination! Six hundred dollars was money enough to make half a dozen boys rich! Here was treasure-hunting under the happiest auspices—there would not be any bothersome uncertainty as to where to dig. They nudged each other every moment—eloquent nudges and easily understood, for they simply meant—"Oh, but ain't you glad *now* we're here!"

Joe's knife struck upon something.

"Hello!" said he.

"What is it?" said his comrade.

"Half-rotten plank—no, it's a box, I believe. Here—bear a hand and we'll see what it's here for. Never mind, I've broke a hole."

He reached his hand in and drew it out—

"Man, it's money!"

The two men examined the handful of coins. They were gold. The boys above were as excited as themselves, and as delighted.

Joe's comrade said:

"We'll make quick work of this. There's an old rusty pick over amongst the weeds in the corner the other side of the fireplace— I saw it a minute ago."

He ran and brought the boys' pick and shovel. Injun Joe took the pick, looked it over critically, shook his head, muttered something to himself, and then began to use it. The box was soon unearthed. It was not very large; it was iron-bound and had been very strong before the slow years had injured it. The men contemplated the treasure awhile in blissful silence.

"Pard, there's thousands of dollars here," said Injun Joe.

" 'Twas always said that Murrel's gang used to be around here one summer," the stranger observed.

"I know it," said Injun Joe; "and this looks like it, I should say."

"*Now* you won't need to do that job."

The half-breed frowned. Said he:

"You don't know me. Least you don't know all about that thing. 'Tain't robbery altogether—it's *revenge!*" and a wicked light flamed in his eyes. "I'll need your help in it. When it's finished—then Texas. Go home to your Nance and your kids, and stand by till you hear from me."

"Well—if you say so. What'll we do with this—bury it again?"

"Yes. [Ravishing delight overhead.] *No!* by the great Sachem, no! [Profound distress overhead.] I'd nearly forgot. That pick had fresh earth on it! [The boys were sick with terror in a moment.] What business has a pick and a shovel here? What business with fresh earth on them? Who brought them here—and where are they gone? Have you heard anybody?—seen anybody? What! bury it again and leave them to come and see the ground disturbed? Not exactly—not exactly. We'll take it to my den."

"Why, of course! Might have thought of that before. You mean Number One?"

"No—Number Two—under the cross. The other place is bad— too common."

"All right. It's nearly dark enough to start."

Injun Joe got up and went about from window to window cautiously peeping out. Presently he said:

"Who could have brought those tools here? Do you reckon they can be up-stairs?"

The boys' breath forsook them. Injun Joe put his hand on his knife, halted a moment, undecided, and then turned toward the stairway. The boys thought of the closet, but their strength was gone. The steps came creaking up the stairs—the intolerable distress of the situation woke the stricken resolution of the lads— they were about to spring for the closet, when there was a crash of rotten timbers and Injun Joe landed on the ground amid the debris of the ruined stairway. He gathered himself up cursing, and his comrade said:

"Now what's the use of all that? If it's anybody, and they're up there, let them *stay* there—who cares? If they want to jump down, now, and get into trouble, who objects? It will be dark in fifteen minutes—and then let them follow us if they want to. I'm willing. In my opinion, whoever hove those things in here caught a sight of us and took us for ghosts or devils or something. I'll bet they're running yet."

Joe grumbled awhile; then he agreed with his friend that what daylight was left ought to be economized in getting things ready for leaving. Shortly afterward they slipped out of the house in the deepening twilight, and moved toward the river with their precious box.

Tom and Huck rose up, weak but vastly relieved, and stared after them through the chinks between the logs of the house. Follow? Not they. They were content to reach ground again without broken necks, and take the townward track over the hill. They did not talk much. They were too much absorbed in hating themselves— hating the ill luck that made them take the spade and the pick there. But for that, Injun Joe never would have suspected. He would have hidden the silver with the gold to wait there till his "revenge" was satisfied, and then he would have had the misfortune to find that money turn up missing. Bitter, bitter luck that the tools were ever brought there!

They resolved to keep a lookout for that Spaniard when he should come to town spying out for chances to do his revengeful job, and follow him to "Number Two," wherever that might be.

The adventure of the day mightily tormented Tom's dreams that night. Four times he had his hands on that rich treasure and four times it wasted to nothingness in his fingers as sleep forsook him and wakefulness brought back the hard reality of his misfortune. As he lay in the early morning recalling the incidents of his great adventure, he noticed that they seemed curiously subdued and far away—somewhat as if they had happened in another world, or in a time long gone by. Then it occurred to him that the great adventure itself must be a dream!

But the incidents of his adventure grew sensibly sharper and clearer under the attrition of thinking them over, and so he presently found himself leaning to the impression that the thing might not have been a dream, after all. This uncertainty must be swept away. He would snatch a hurried breakfast and go find Huck.

Huck was sitting on the gunwale of a flatboat, listlessly dangling his feet in the water and looking very melancholy. Tom concluded to let Huck lead up to the subject. If he did not do it, then the adventure would be proved to have been only a dream.

"Hello, Huck!"

"Hello, yourself."

Silence for a minute.

"Tom, if we'd 'a' left the blame tools at the dead tree, we'd 'a' got the money. Oh, ain't it awful!"

"'Tain't a dream, then, 'tain't a dream! Somehow I most wish it was. Dog'd if I don't, Huck."

"What ain't a dream?"

"Oh, that thing yesterday. I been half thinking it was."

"Dream! If them stairs hadn't broke down you'd 'a' seen how

much dream it was! I've had dreams enough all night—with that patch-eyed Spanish devil going for me all through 'em—rot him!"

"No, not rot him. *Find* him! Track the money!"

"Tom, we'll never find him. A feller don't have only one chance for such a pile—and that one's lost. I'd feel mighty shaky if I was to see him, anyway."

"Well, so'd I; but I'd like to see him, anyway—and track him out—to his Number Two."

"Number Two—yes, that's it. I ben thinking 'bout that. But I can't make nothing out of it. What do you reckon it is?"

"I dono. It's too deep. Say, Huck—maybe it's the number of a house!"

"Goody! . . . No, Tom, that ain't it. If it is, it ain't in this one-horse town. They ain't no numbers here."

"Well, that's so. Lemme think a minute. Here—it's the number of a room—in a tavern, you know!"

"Oh, that's the trick! They ain't only two taverns. We can find out quick."

"You stay here, Huck, till I come."

Tom was off at once. He did not care to have Huck's company in public places. He was gone half an hour. He found that in the best tavern, No. 2 had long been occupied by a young lawyer, and was still so occupied. In the less ostentatious house No. 2 was a mystery. The tavern-keeper's young son said it was kept locked all the time, and he never saw anybody go into it or come out of it except at night; he did not know any particular reason for this state of things; had had some little curiosity, but it was rather feeble; had made the most of the mystery by entertaining himself with the idea that that room was "ha'nted"; had noticed that there was a light in there the night before.

"That's what I've found out, Huck. I reckon that's the very No. 2 we're after."

"I reckon it is, Tom. Now what you going to do?"

"Lemme think."

Tom thought a long time. Then he said:

"I'll tell you. The back door of that No. 2 is the door that comes out into that little close alley between the tavern and the old rattle-trap of a brick store. Now you get hold of all the doorkeys you can find, and I'll nip all of auntie's, and the first dark night we'll go there and try 'em. And mind you, keep a lookout for Injun Joe, because he said he was going to drop into town and spy around once more for a chance to get his revenge. If you see him, you just follow him; and if he don't go to that No. 2, that ain't the place."

"Lordy, I don't want to foller him by myself!"

"You bet *I*'ll follow him, if it's dark, Huck. Why, he might 'a' found out he couldn't get his revenge, and be going right after that money."

"It's so, Tom, it's so. I'll foller him; I will, by jingoes!"

"Now, you're *talking!* Don't you ever weaken, Huck, and I won't."

That night Tom and Huck were ready for their adventure. They hung about the neighborhood of the tavern until after nine, one watching the alley at a distance and the other the tavern door. Nobody entered the alley or left it; nobody resembling the Spaniard entered or left the tavern door. The night promised to be a fair one; so Tom went home with the understanding that if a considerable degree of darkness came on, Huck was to come and "maow," whereupon he would slip out and try the keys. But the night remained clear, and Huck closed his watch and retired to bed in an empty sugar hogshead about twelve.

Tuesday the boys had the same ill luck. Also Wednesday. But Thursday night promised better. Tom slipped out in good season with his aunt's old tin lantern, and a large towel to blindfold it with. He hid the lantern in Huck's sugar hogshead and the watch began. An hour before midnight the tavern closed up and its lights (the only ones thereabouts) were put out. No Spaniard had been seen. Nobody had entered or left the alley. Everything was auspicious. The blackness of darkness reigned, the perfect stillness was interrupted only by occasional mutterings of distant thunder.

Tom got his lantern, lit it in the hogshead, wrapped it closely in the towel, and the two adventurers crept in the gloom toward the tavern. Huck stood sentry and Tom felt his way into the alley. Then there was a season of waiting anxiety that weighed upon Huck's spirits like a mountain. Suddenly there was a flash of light and Tom came tearing by him:

"Run!" said he; "run for your life!"

He needn't have repeated it; once was enough; Huck was making thirty or forty miles an hour before the repetition was uttered. The boys never stopped till they reached the shed of a deserted slaughter-house at the lower end of the village. Just as they got within its shelter the storm burst and the rain poured down. As soon as Tom got his breath he said:

"Huck, it was awful! I tried two of the keys, just as soft as I could; but they seemed to make such a power of racket that I couldn't hardly get my breath I was so scared. They wouldn't turn in the lock, either. Well, without noticing what I was doing, I took hold of the knob, and open comes the door! It warn't locked! I hopped in, and shook off the towel, and, *great Cæsar's ghost!*"

"What—what'd you see, Tom?"

"Huck, I most stepped onto Injun Joe's hand!"

"No!"

"Yes! He was laying there, sound asleep on the floor, with his old patch on his eye and his arms spread out."

"Lordy, what did you do? Did he wake up?"

"No, never budged. Drunk, I reckon. I just grabbed that towel and started!"

"I'd never 'a' thought of the towel, I bet!"

"Well, *I* would. My aunt would make me mighty sick if I lost it."

"Say, Tom, did you see that box?"

"Huck, I didn't wait to look around. I didn't see the box, I didn't see the cross. I didn't see anything but a bottle and a tin cup on the floor by Injun Joe; yes, and I saw two barrels and lots more bottles in the room. Don't you see, now, what's the matter with that ha'nted room?"

"How?"

"Why, it's ha'nted with whisky! Maybe *all* the Temperance Taverns have got a ha'nted room, hey, Huck?"

"Well, I reckon maybe that's so. Who'd 'a' thought such a thing? But say, Tom, now's a mighty good time to get that box, if Injun Joe's drunk."

"It is that! You try it!"

Huck shuddered.

"Well, no—I reckon not."

"And *I* reckon not, Huck. Only one bottle alongside of Injun Joe ain't enough. If there'd been three, he'd be drunk enough and I'd do it."

There was a long pause for reflection, and then Tom said:

"Lookyhere, Huck, le's not try that thing any more till we know Injun Joe's not in there. It's too scary. Now, if we watch every night, we'll be dead sure to see him go out, some time or other, and then we'll snatch that box quicker'n lightning."

"Well, I'm agreed. I'll watch the whole night long, and I'll do it every night, too, if you'll do the other part of the job."

"All right, I will. All you got to do is to trot up Hooper Street a block and maow—and if I'm asleep, you throw some gravel at the window and that'll fetch me."

"Agreed, and good as wheat!"

The first thing Tom heard on Friday morning was a glad piece of news—Judge Thatcher's family had come back to town the night before. Both Injun Joe and the treasure sank into secondary importance for a moment, and Becky took the chief place in the boy's interest. He saw her, and they had an exhausting good time playing "hi-spy" and "gully-keeper" with a crowd of their school-mates. The day was completed and crowned in a peculiarly satis-factory way: Becky teased her mother to appoint the next day for the long-promised and long-delayed picnic, and she consented. The child's delight was boundless; and Tom's not more moderate. The invitations were sent out before sunset, and straightway the young folks of the village were thrown into a fever of preparation and pleasurable anticipation. Tom's excitement enabled him to keep awake until a pretty late hour, and he had good hopes of hearing Huck's "maow," and of having his treasure to astonish Becky and the picnickers with, next day; but he was disappointed. No signal came that night.

Morning came, eventually, and by ten or eleven o'clock a giddy and rollicking company were gathered at Judge Thatcher's, and everything was ready for a start. It was not the custom for elderly people to mar picnics with their presence. The children were considered safe enough under the wings of a few young ladies of eighteen and a few young gentlemen of twenty-three or thereabouts. The old steam-ferryboat was chartered for the occasion; presently the gay throng filed up the main street laden with provision-baskets. The last thing Mrs. Thatcher said to Becky was:

"You'll not get back till late. Perhaps you'd better stay all night with some of the girls that live near the ferry landing, child."

"Then I'll stay with Suzy Harper, mamma."

"Very well. And mind and behave yourself and don't be any trouble."

Presently, as they tripped along, Tom said to Becky:

"Say I'll tell you what we'll do. 'Stead of going to Joe Harper's we'll climb right up the hill and stop at the Widow Douglas's. She'll have ice-cream! She has it most every day—dead loads of it. And she'll be awful glad to have us."

"Oh, that will be fun!"

Then Becky reflected a moment and said:

"But what will mamma say?"

"How'll she ever know?"

The girl turned the idea over in her mind, and said reluctantly:

"I reckon it's wrong—but——"

"But shucks! Your mother won't know, and so what's the harm? All she wants is that you'll be safe; and I bet you she'd 'a' said go there if she'd 'a' thought of it. I know she would!"

The Widow Douglas's splendid hospitality was a tempting bait. It and Tom's persuasions presently carried the day. So it was decided to say nothing to anybody about the night's program. Presently it occurred to Tom that maybe Huck might come this very night and give the signal. The thought took a deal of the spirit out of his anticipations. Still he could not bear to give up the fun at Widow Douglas's. And why should he give it up, he reasoned—the signal did not come the night before, so why should it be any more likely to come to-night? The sure fun of the evening outweighed the uncertain treasure; and boy-like, he determined to yield to the stronger inclination and not allow himself to think of the box of money another time that day.

Three miles below town the ferryboat stopped at the mouth of a woody hollow and tied up. The crowd swarmed ashore and soon the forest distances and craggy heights echoed far and near with shoutings and laughter. All the different ways of getting hot and tired were gone through with, and by and by the rovers straggled back to camp fortified with responsible appetites, and then the destruction of the good things began. After the feast there was a refreshing season of rest and chat in the shade of spreading oaks. By and by somebody shouted:

"Who's ready for the cave?"

Everybody was. Bundles of candles were procured, and straightway there was a general scamper up the hill. The mouth of the cave was up the hillside—an opening shaped like a letter A. Its massive oaken door stood unbarred. Within was a small chamber, chilly as an icehouse, and walled by Nature with solid limestone that was dewy with a cold sweat. It was romantic and mysterious to stand here in the deep gloom and look out upon the green valley shining in the sun. But the impressiveness of the situation quickly wore off, and the romping began again. The moment a candle was lighted there was a general rush upon the owner of it; a struggle and a gallant defense followed, but the candle was soon knocked down or blown out, and then there was a glad clamor of laughter and a new chase. But all things have an end. By and by the procession went filing down the steep descent of the main avenue, the flickering rank of lights dimly revealing the lofty walls of rock almost to their point of junction sixty feet overhead. This main avenue was not more than eight or ten feet wide. Every few steps other lofty and still narrower crevices branched from it on either hand—for McDougal's cave was but a vast labyrinth of crooked aisles that ran into each other and out again and led nowhere. It was said that one might wander days and nights together through its intricate tangle of rifts and chasms, and never find the end of the cave; and that he might go down and down, and still down, into the earth, and it was just the same—labyrinth, underneath labyrinth, and no end to any of them. No man "knew" the cave. That was an impossible thing. Most of the young men knew a portion of it, and it was not customary to venture much beyond this known portion. Tow Sawyer knew as much of the cave as any one.

The procession moved along the main avenue some three-quarters of a mile, and then groups and couples began to slip aside into branch avenues, fly along the dismal corridors, and take each other by surprise at points where the corridors joined again. Parties were able to elude each other for the space of half an hour without going beyond the "known" ground.

By and by, one group after another came straggling back to the mouth of the cave, panting, hilarious, smeared from head to foot with tallow drippings, daubed with clay, and entirely delighted with the success of the day. Then they were astonished to find that they had been taking no note of time and that night was about at hand. The clanging bell had been calling for half an hour. However, this sort of close to the day's adventures was romantic and therefore satisfactory. When the ferryboat with her wild freight pushed into the stream, nobody cared sixpence for the wasted time but the captain of the craft.

Huck was already upon his watch when the ferryboat's lights went glinting past the wharf. He heard no noise on board, for the young people were as subdued and still as people usually are who are nearly tired to death. He wondered what boat it was, and why she did not stop at the wharf—and then he dropped her out of his

mind and put his attention upon his business. The night was growing cloudy and dark. Ten o'clock came, and the noise of vehicles
ceased, scattered lights began to wink out, all straggling foot-
passengers disappeared, the village betook itself to its slumbers and
left the small watcher alone with the silence and the ghosts. Eleven
o'clock came, and the tavern lights were put out; darkness everywhere, now. Huck waited what seemed a weary long time, but
nothing happened. His faith was weakening. Was there any use?
Was there really any use? Why not give it up and turn in?

A noise fell upon his ear. He was all attention in an instant.
The alley door closed softly. He sprang to the corner of the brick
store. The next moment two men brushed by him, and one seemed
to have something under his arm. It must be that box! So they
were going to remove the treasure. Why call Tom now? It would
be absurd—the men would get away with the box and never be
found again. No, he would stick to their wake and follow them;
he would trust to the darkness for security from discovery. So
communing with himself, Huck stepped out and glided along behind the men, catlike, with bare feet, allowing them to keep just
far enough ahead not to be invisible.

They moved up the river street three blocks, then turned to the
left up a cross-street. They went straight ahead, then, until they
came to the path that led up Cardiff Hill; this they took. They
plunged into the narrow path between the tall sumach bushes,
and were at once hidden in the gloom. Huck closed up and
shortened his distance, now, for they would never be able to see
him. He trotted along awhile; then slackened his pace, fearing he
was gaining too fast; moved on a piece, then stopped altogether;
listened; no sound; none, save that he seemed to hear the beating
of his own heart. The hooting of an owl came from over the hill—
ominous sound! But no footsteps. Heavens, was everything lost!
He was about to spring with winged feet, when a man cleared his
throat not four feet from him! Huck's heart shot into his throat,
but he swallowed it again; and then he stood there shaking as if a
dozen agues had taken charge of him at once, and so weak that

he thought he must surely fall to the ground. He knew where he was. He knew he was within five steps of the stile leading into Widow Douglas's grounds. Very well, he thought, let them bury it there; it won't be hard to find.

Now there was a voice—a very low voice—Injun Joe's:

"Maybe she's got company—there's lights, late as it is."

"I can't see any."

"Because the bush is in your way. Now—this way—now you see, don't you?"

"Yes. Well, there *is* company there, I reckon. Better give it up."

"Give it up, and I just leaving this country forever! Give it up and maybe never have another chance. I tell you again, as I've told you before, I don't care for her swag—you may have it. But her husband was rough on me—many times he was rough on me —and mainly he was the justice of the peace that jugged me for a vagrant. And that ain't all. It ain't a millionth part of it! He had me *horsewhipped!*—horsewhipped in front of the jail—with all the town looking on! HORSEWHIPPED!—do you understand? He took advantage of me and died. But I'll take it out of *her.*"

"Oh, don't kill her! Don't do that!"

"Kill? Who said anything about killing? I would kill *him* if he was here; but not her. When you want to get revenge on a woman you don't kill her—bosh! you go for her looks. You slit her nostrils —you notch her ears like a sow!"

"By God, that's——"

"Keep your opinion to yourself! It will be safest for you. I'll tie her to the bed. If she bleeds to death, is that my fault? I'll not cry, if she does. My friend, you'll help in this thing—for *my* sake— that's why you're here—I mightn't be able alone. If you flinch, I'll kill you. Do you understand that? And if I have to kill you, I'll kill her—and then I reckon nobody'll ever know much about who done this business."

"Well, if it's got to be done, let's get at it. The quicker the bet- ter—I'm all in a shiver."

"Do it *now?* And company there? Look here—I'll get suspicious of you, first thing you know. No—we'll wait till the lights are out —there's no hurry."

Huck felt that a silence was going to ensue—a thing still more awful than any amount of murderous talk; so he held his breath and stepped gingerly back; planted his foot carefully and firmly, after balancing, one-legged, in a precarious way and almost toppling over, first on one side and then on the other. He took another step back, with the same elaboration and the same risks; then another and another, and—a twig snapped under his foot! His breath stopped and he listened. There was no sound—the stillness was perfect. His gratitude was measureless. Now he turned in his tracks, between the walls of sumach bushes—turned himself as carefully as if he were a ship—and then stepped quickly but cautiously along. When he emerged at the quarry he felt secure, and so he picked up his nimble heels and flew. Down, down he sped, till he reached the Welshman's. He banged at the door, and presently the heads of the old man and his two stalwart sons were thrust from windows.

"What's the row there? Who's banging? What do you want?"

"Let me in—quick! I'll tell everything."

"Why, who are you?"

"Huckleberry Finn—quick, let me in!"

"Huckleberry Finn, indeed! It ain't a name to open many doors, I judge! But let him in, lads, and let's see what's the trouble."

"Please don't ever tell *I* told you," were Huck's first words when he got in. "Please don't—I'd be killed, sure—but the widow's been good friends to me sometimes, and I want to tell—I *will* tell if you'll promise you won't ever say it was me."

"By George, he *has* got something to tell, or he wouldn't act so!" exclaimed the old man; "out with it and nobody here'll ever tell, lad."

Three minutes later the old man and his sons, well armed, were up the hill, and just entering the sumach path on tiptoe, their weapons in their hands. Huck accompanied them no farther. He hid behind a great boulder and fell to listening. There was a lagging, anxious silence, and then all of a sudden there was an explosion of firearms and a cry.

Huck waited for no particulars. He sprang away and sped down the hill as fast as his legs could carry him.

As the earliest suspicion of dawn appeared on Sunday morning, Huck came groping up the hill and rapped gently at the old Welshman's door. The inmates were asleep, but it was a sleep that was set on a hair-trigger, on account of the exciting episode of the night. A call came from a window:

"Who's there!"

Huck's scared voice answered in a low tone:

"Please let me in! It's only Huck Finn!"

"It's a name that can open this door night or day, lad!—and welcome!"

These were strange words to the vagabond boy's ears, and the pleasantest he had ever heard. He could not recollect that the closing word had ever been applied in his case before. The door was quickly unlocked, and he entered. Huck was given a seat and the old man and his brace of tall sons speedily dressed themselves.

"Now, my boy, I hope you're good and hungry, because breakfast will be ready as soon as the sun's up, and we'll have a piping hot one, too—make yourself easy about that! I and the boys hoped you'd turn up and stop here last night."

"I was awful scared," said Huck, "and I run. I took out when the pistols went off, and I didn't stop for three mile. I've come now becuz I wanted to know about it, you know; and I come before daylight becuz I didn't want to run acrost them devils, even if they was dead."

"Well, poor chap, you do look as if you'd had a hard night of it —but there's a bed here for you when you've had your breakfast. No, they ain't dead, lad—we are sorry enough for that. You see we knew right where to put our hands on them, by your description; so we crept along on tiptoe till we got within fifteen feet of them—dark as a cellar that sumach path was—and just then

I was going to sneeze. It was the meanest kind of luck! I tried to keep it back, but no use—'twas bound to come, and it did come! I was in the lead with my pistol raised, and when the sneeze started those scoundrels a-rustling to get out of the path, I sung out, 'Fire, boys!' and blazed away at the place where the rustling was. So did the boys. But they were off in a jiffy, those villains, and we after them, down through the woods. I judge we never touched them. They fired a shot apiece as they started, but their bullets whizzed by and didn't do us any harm. As soon as we lost the sound of their feet we quit chasing, and went down and stirred up the constables. They got a posse together, and went off to guard the river-bank, and as soon as it is light the sheriff and a gang are going to beat up the woods. My boys will be with them presently. I wish we had some sort of description of those rascals— 'twould help a good deal. But you couldn't see what they were like, in the dark, lad, I suppose?"

"Oh, yes, I saw them down-town and follered them."

"Splendid! Describe them—describe them, my boy!"

"One's the old deaf and dumb Spaniard that's ben around here once or twice, and t'other's a mean-looking, ragged——"

"That's enough, lad, we know the men! Happened on them in the woods back of the widow's one day, and they slunk away. Off with you, boys, and tell the sheriff—get your breakfast to-morrow morning!"

The Welshman's sons departed at once. As they were leaving the room Huck sprang up and exclaimed:

"Oh, please don't tell *any*body it was me that blowed on them! Oh, please!"

"All right if you say it, Huck, but you ought to have the credit of what you did."

"Oh, no, no! Please don't tell!"

When the young men were gone, the old Welshman said:

"They won't tell—and I won't. But why don't you want it known?"

Huck would not explain, further than to say that he already

knew too much about one of those men and would not have the man know that he knew anything against him for the whole world —he would be killed for knowing it, sure.

The old man promised secrecy once more, and said:

"How did you come to follow these fellows, lad? Were they looking suspicious?"

Huck was silent while he framed a duly cautious reply. Then he said:

"Well, you see, I'm a kind of a hard lot—least everybody says so, and I don't see nothing agin it—and sometimes I can't sleep much on accounts of thinking about it and sort of trying to strike out a new way of doing. That was the way of it last night. I couldn't sleep, and so I come along up street 'bout midnight, a-turning it all over, and when I got to that old shackly brick store by the Temperance Tavern, I backed up again the wall to have another think. Well, just then along comes these two chaps slipping along close by me, with something under their arm and I reckoned they'd stole it. One was a-smoking, and t'other one wanted a light; so they stopped right before me and the cigars lit up their faces and I see that the big one was the deaf and dumb Spaniard, by his white whiskers and the patch on his eye, and t'other one was a rusty, ragged-looking devil."

"Could you see the rags by the light of the cigars?"

This staggered Huck for a moment. Then he said:

"Well, I don't know—but somehow it seems as if I did."

"Then they went on, and you——"

"Follered 'em—yes. That was it. I wanted to see what was up— they sneaked along so. I dogged 'em to the widder's stile, and stood in the dark and heard the ragged one beg for the widder, and the Spaniard swear he'd spile her looks just as I told you and your two——"

"What! The *deaf and dumb* man said all that!"

Huck had made another terrible mistake! He was trying his best to keep the old man from getting the faintest hint of who the

Spaniard might be, and yet his tongue seemed determined to get him into trouble in spite of all he could do. He made several efforts to creep out of his scrape, but the old man's eye was upon him and he made blunder after blunder. Presently the Welshman said:

"My boy, don't be afraid of me. I wouldn't hurt a hair of your head for all the world. No—I'd protect you—I'd protect you. This Spaniard is not deaf and dumb; you've let that slip without intending it; you can't cover that up now. You know something about that Spaniard that you want to keep dark. Now trust me— tell me what it is, and trust me—I won't betray you."

Huck looked into the old man's honest eyes a moment, then bent over and whispered in his ear:

" 'Tain't a Spaniard—it's Injun Joe!"

The Welshman almost jumped out of his chair. In a moment he said:

"It's all plain enough, now. When you talked about notching ears and slitting noses I judged that that was your own embellishment, because white men don't take that sort of revenge. But an Injun! That's a different matter altogether."

During breakfast the talk went on, and in the course of it the old man said that the last thing which he and his sons had done, before going to bed, was to get a lantern and examine the stile and its vicinity for marks of blood. They found none, but captured a bulky bundle of——"

"Of WHAT?"

If the words had been lightning they could not have leaped with a more stunning suddenness from Huck's blanched lips. His eyes were staring wide, now, and his breath suspended—waiting for the answer. The Welshman started—stared in return—three seconds—five seconds—ten—then replied:

"Of burglar's tools. Why, what's the *matter* with you?"

Huck sank back, panting gently, but deeply, unutterably grateful. The Welshman eyed him gravely, curiously—and presently said:

"Yes, burglar's tools. That appears to relieve you a good deal. But what did give you that turn? What were *you* expecting we'd found?"

Huck was in a close place—the inquiring eye was upon him—he would have given anything for material for a plausible answer—nothing suggested itself—the inquiring eye was boring deeper and deeper—a senseless reply offered—there was no time to weigh it, so at a venture he uttered it—feebly:

"Sunday-school books, maybe."

Poor Huck was too distressed to smile, but the old man laughed loud and joyously, shook up the details of his anatomy from head to foot, and ended by saying that such a laugh was money in a man's pocket, because it cut down the doctor's bills like everything. Then he added:

"Poor old chap, you're white and jaded—you ain't well a bit—no wonder you're a little flighty and off your balance. But you'll come out of it. Rest and sleep will fetch you out all right, I hope."

Huck was irritated to think he had been such a goose and betrayed such a suspicious excitement, for he had dropped the idea that the parcel brought from the tavern was the treasure, as soon as he had heard the talk at the widow's stile. He had only *thought* it was not the treasure, however—he had not known that it wasn't—and so the suggestion of a captured bundle was too much for his self-possession. But on the whole he felt glad the little episode had happened, for now he knew beyond all question that that bundle was not *the* bundle, and so his mind was at rest and exceedingly comfortable. In fact, everything seemed to be drifting just in the right direction, now; the treasure must be still in No. 2, the men would be captured and jailed that day, and he and Tom could seize the gold that night without any trouble or any fear of interruption.

Just as breakfast was completed there was a knock at the door. Huck jumped for a hiding-place, for he had no mind to be connected even remotely with the late event. The Welshman admitted several ladies and gentlemen, among them the Widow Douglas, and noticed that groups of citizens were climbing up the hill—to stare at the stile. So the news had spread.

The Welshman had to tell the story of the night to the visitors. The widow's gratitude for her preservation was outspoken.

"Don't say a word about it, madam. There's another that you're more beholden to than you are to me and my boys, maybe, but he don't allow me to tell his name. We wouldn't have been there but for him."

Of course this excited a curiosity so vast that it almost belittled the main matter—but the Welshman allowed it to eat into the vitals of his visitors, and through them be transmitted to the whole town, for he refused to part with his secret. When all else had been learned, the widow said:

"I went to sleep reading in bed and slept straight through all that noise. Why didn't you come and wake me?"

"We judged it warn't worth while. Those fellows warn't likely to come again—they hadn't any tools left to work with, and what was the use of waking you up and scaring you to death? My three negro men stood guard at your house all the rest of the night. They've just come back."

More visitors came, and the story had to be told and retold for a couple of hours more.

There was no Sabbath-school during day-school vacation, but everybody was early at church. The stirring event was well canvassed. News came that not a sign of the two villains had been yet discovered. When the sermon was finished, Judge Thatcher's wife dropped alongside of Mrs. Harper as she moved down the aisle with the crowd and said:

"Is my Becky going to sleep all day? I just expected she would be tired to death."

"Your Becky?"

"Yes," with a startled look—"didn't she stay with you last night?"

"Why, no."

Mrs. Thatcher turned pale, and sank into a pew, just as Aunt Polly, talking briskly with a friend, passed by. Aunt Polly said:

"Good morning, Mrs. Thatcher. Good morning, Mrs. Harper. I've got a boy that's turned up missing. I reckon my Tom stayed at your house last night—one of you. And now he's afraid to come to church. I've got to settle with him."

Mrs. Thatcher shook her head feebly and turned paler than ever.

"He didn't stay with us," said Mrs. Harper beginning to look uneasy. A marked anxiety came into Aunt Polly's face.

"Joe Harper, have you seen my Tom this morning?"

"No'm."

"When did you see him last?"

Joe tried to remember, but was not sure he could say. The people had stopped moving out of church. Whispers passed along, and a boding uneasiness took possession of every countenance. Children were anxiously questioned, and young teachers. They all said they had not noticed whether Tom and Becky were on board the ferryboat on the homeward trip; it was dark; no one thought of inquiring if any one was missing. One young man finally blurted out his fear that they were still in the cave! Mrs. Thatcher swooned away. Aunt Polly fell to crying and wringing her hands.

The alarm swept from lip to lip, from group to group, from street to street, and within five minutes the bells were wildly clanging and the whole town was up! The Cardiff Hill episode sank into instant insignificance, the burglars were forgotten, horses were saddled, skiffs were manned, the ferryboat ordered out, and before the horror was half an hour old two hundred men were pouring down highroad and river toward the cave.

All the long afternoon the village seemed empty and dead. Many women visited Aunt Polly and Mrs. Thatcher and tried to comfort them. They cried with them, too, and that was still better than words. All the tedious night the town waited for news; but when the morning dawned at last, all the word that came was, "Send more candles—and send food." Mrs. Thatcher was almost crazed; and Aunt Polly, also. Judge Thatcher sent messages of hope and encouragement from the cave, but they conveyed no real cheer.

The old Welshman came home toward daylight, spattered with

candle-grease, smeared with clay, and almost worn out. He found Huck still in the bed that had been provided for him, and delirious with fever. The physicians were all at the cave, so the Widow Douglas came and took charge of the patient. She said she would do her best by him, because, whether he was good, bad, or indifferent, he was the Lord's, and nothing that was the Lord's was a thing to be neglected. The Welshman said Huck had good spots in him, and the widow said:

"You can depend on it. That's the Lord's mark. He don't leave it off. He never does. Puts it somewhere on every creature that comes from His hands."

Early in the forenoon parties of jaded men began to straggle into the village, but the strongest of the citizens continued searching. All the news that could be gained was that remotenesses of the cavern were being ransacked that had never been visited before; that every corner and crevice was going to be thoroughly searched; that wherever one wandered through the maze of passages, lights were to be seen flitting hither and thither in the distance, and shoutings and pistol-shots sent their hollow reverberations to the ear down the somber aisles. In one place, far from the section usually traversed by tourists, the names "Becky & Tom" had been found traced upon the rocky wall with candlesmoke, and near at hand a grease-soiled bit of ribbon. Mrs. Thatcher recognized the ribbon and cried over it. She said it was the last relic she should ever have of her child; and that no other memorial of her could ever be so precious, because this one parted latest from the living body before the awful death came. Some said that now and then, in the cave, a faraway speck of light would glimmer, and then a glorious shout would burst forth and a score of men go trooping down the echoing aisle—and then a sickening disappointment always followed; the children were not there; it was only a searcher's light.

Three dreadful days and nights dragged their tedious hours along, and the village sank into a hopeless stupor. No one had heart for anything.

Now to return to Tom and Becky's share in the picnic. They tripped along the murky aisles with the rest of the company, visiting the familiar wonders of the cave—wonders dubbed with rather over-descriptive names, such as "The Drawing-Room," "The Cathedral," "Aladdin's Palace," and so on. Presently the hide-and-seek frolicking began, and Tom and Becky engaged in it with zeal until the exertion began to grow a trifle wearisome; then they wandered down a sinuous avenue holding their candles aloft and reading the tangled web-work of names, dates, post-office addresses, and mottoes with which the rocky walls had been frescoed (in candle-smoke). Still drifting along and talking, they scarcely noticed that they were now in a part of the cave whose walls were not frescoed. They smoked their own names under an overhanging shelf and moved on. Presently they came to a place where a little stream of water, trickling over a ledge and carrying a limestone sediment with it, had, in the slow-dragging ages, formed a laced and ruffled Niagara in gleaming and imperishable stone. Tom squeezed his small body behind it in order to illuminate it for Becky's gratification. He found that it curtained a sort of steep natural stairway which was inclosed between narrow walls, and at once the ambition to be a discoverer seized him. Becky responded to his call, and they made a smoke-mark for future guidance, and started upon their quest. They wound this way and that, far down into the secret depths of the cave, made another mark, and branched off in search of novelties to tell the upper world about. In one place they found a spacious cavern, from whose ceiling depended a multitude of shining stalactites of the length and circumference of a man's leg; they walked all about it, wondering and admiring, and presently left it by one of the numerous passages that opened into it. This shortly brought them to a bewitching spring, whose basin was incrusted with a frostwork of glittering crystals; it was in the midst of a cavern whose walls were supported by many fantastic pillars which had been formed by the joining of great stalactites and stalagmites together, the result of the

ceaseless water-drip of centuries. Under the roof vast knots of bats had packed themselves together, thousands in a bunch; the lights disturbed the creatures, and they came flocking down by hundreds, squeaking and darting furiously at the candles. Tom knew their ways and the danger of this sort of conduct. He seized Becky's hand and hurried her into the first corridor that offered; and none too soon, for a bat struck Becky's light out with its wing while she was passing out of the cavern. The bats chased the children a good distance; but the fugitives plunged into every new passage that offered, and at last got rid of the perilous things. Tom found a subterranean lake, shortly, which stretched its dim length away until its shape was lost in the shadows. He wanted to explore its borders, but concluded that it would be best to sit down and rest awhile, first. Now, for the first time, the deep stillness of the place laid a clammy hand upon the spirits of the children. Becky said:

"Why, I didn't notice, but it seems ever so long since I heard of any of the others."

"Come to think, Becky, we are away down below them—and I don't know how far away north, or south, or east, or whichever it is. We couldn't hear them here."

Becky grew apprehensive.

"I wonder how long we've been down here, Tom. We better start back."

"Yes, I reckon we better. P'raps we better."

"Can you find the way, Tom? It's all a mixed-up crookedness to me."

"I reckon I could find it—but then the bats. If they put both our candles out it will be an awful fix. Let's try some other way, so as not to go through there."

"Well. But I hope we won't get lost. It would be so awful!" and the girl shuddered at the thought of the dreadful possibilities.

They started through a corridor, and traversed it in silence a long way, glancing at each new opening to see if there was anything familiar about the look of it; but they were all strange. Every time Tom made an examination, Becky would watch his face for an encouraging sign, and he would say cheerily:

"Oh, it's all right. This ain't the one, but we'll come to it right away!"

But he felt less and less hopeful with each failure, and presently began to turn off into diverging avenues at sheer random, in desperate hope of finding the one that was wanted. He still said it was "all right," but there was such a leaden dread at his heart that the words had lost their ring and sounded just as if he had said, "All is lost!" Becky clung to his side in an anguish of fear, and tried hard to keep back the tears, but they would come. At last she said:

"Oh, Tom, never mind the bats, let's go back that way! We seem to get worse and worse off all the time."

Tom stopped.

"Listen!" said he.

Profound silence; silence so deep that even their breathings were conspicuous in the hush. Tom shouted. The call went echoing down the empty aisles and died out in the distance in a faint sound that resembled a ripple of mocking laughter.

"Oh, don't do it again, Tom, it is too horrid," said Becky.

"It is horrid, but I better, Becky; they *might* hear us, you know," and he shouted again.

The "might" was even a chillier horror than the ghostly laughter, it so confessed a perishing hope. The children stood still and listened; but there was no result. Tom turned upon the back track at once, and hurried his steps. It was but a little while before a certain indecision in his manner revealed another fearful fact to Becky—he could not find his way back!

"Oh, Tom, you didn't make any marks!"

"Becky, I was such a fool! Such a fool! I never thought we might want to come back! No—I can't find the way. It's all mixed up."

"Tom, Tom, we're lost! we're lost! We never can get out of this awful place! Oh, why *did* we ever leave the others!"

She sank to the ground and burst into such a frenzy of crying that Tom was appalled with the idea that she might die, or lose her reason. He sat down by her and put his arms around her; she buried her face in his bosom, she clung to him, she poured out her terrors, her unavailing regrets, and the far echoes turned them all to jeering laughter. Tom begged her to pluck up hope again, and she said she could not. He fell to blaming and abusing himself for getting her into this miserable situation; this had a better effect. She said she would try to hope again, she would get up and follow wherever he might lead if only he would not talk like that any more. For he was no more to blame than she, she said.

So they moved on again—aimlessly—simply at random—all they could do was to move, keep moving. For a little while, hope made a show of reviving—not with any reason to back it, but only because it is its nature to revive when the spring has not been taken out of it by age and familiarity with failure.

By and by Tom took Becky's candle and blew it out. This economy meant so much! Words were not needed. Becky understood, and her hope died again. She knew that Tom had a whole candle and three or four pieces in his pockets—yet he must economize.

By and by, fatigue began to assert its claims; the children tried to pay no attention, for it was dreadful to think of sitting down when time was grown to be so precious; moving, in some direction, in any direction, was at least progress and might bear fruit; but to sit down was to invite death and shorten its pursuit.

At last Becky's frail limbs refused to carry her farther. She sat down. Tom rested with her, and they talked of home, and the friends there, and the comfortable beds and, above all, the light! Becky cried, and Tom tried to think of some way of comforting her, but all his encouragements were grown threadbare with use, and sounded like sarcasms. Fatigue bore so heavily upon Becky that she drowsed off to sleep. Tom was grateful. He sat looking into her drawn face and saw it grow smooth and natural under the influence of pleasant dreams; and by and by a smile dawned and rested there. The peaceful face reflected somewhat of peace and healing into his own spirit, and his thoughts wandered away to bygone times and dreamy memories. While he was deep in his musings, Becky woke up with a breezy little laugh—but it was stricken dead upon her lips, and a groan followed it.

"Oh, how *could* I sleep! I wish I never, never had waked! No! No, I don't, Tom! Don't look so! I won't say it again."

"I'm glad you've slept, Becky; you'll feel rested, now, and we'll find the way out."

"We can try, Tom; but I've seen such a beautiful country in my dream. I reckon we are going there."

"Maybe not, maybe not. Cheer up, Becky, and let's go on trying."

They rose up and wandered along, hand in hand and hopeless. They tried to estimate how long they had been in the cave, but all they knew was that it seemed days and weeks, and yet it was plain that this could not be, for their candles were not gone yet. A long time after this—they could not tell how long—Tom said they must go softly and listen for dripping water—they must find a spring. They found one presently, and Tom said it was time to rest again. Both were cruelly tired, yet Becky said she thought she could go on a little farther. She was surprised to hear Tom dissent. She could not understand it. They sat down, and Tom fastened his candle to the wall in front of them with some clay. Thought was soon busy; nothing was said for some time. Then Becky broke the silence:

"Tom, I am so hungry!"

Tom took something out of his pocket.

"Do you remember this?" said he.

Becky almost smiled.

"It's our wedding-cake, Tom."

"Yes—I wish it was as big as a barrel, for it's all we've got."

"I saved it from the picnic for us to dream on, Tom, the way grown-up people do with wedding-cake—but it'll be our——"

She dropped the sentence where it was. Tom divided the cake and Becky ate with good appetite, while Tom nibbled at his moiety. There was abundance of cold water to finish the feast with. By and by Becky suggested that they move on again. Tom was silent a moment. Then he said:

"Becky, can you bear it if I tell you something?"

Becky's face paled, but she thought she could.

"Well, then, Becky, we must stay here, where there's water to drink. That little piece is our last candle!"

Becky gave loose to tears and wailings. Tom did what he could to comfort her, but with little effect. At length Becky said:

"Tom!"

"Well, Becky?"

"They'll miss us and hunt for us!"

"Yes, they will! Certainly they will!"

"Maybe they're hunting for us now, Tom."

"Why, I reckon maybe they are. I hope they are."

"When would they miss us, Tom?"

"When they get back to the boat, I reckon."

"Tom, it might be dark then—would they notice we hadn't come?"

"I don't know. But anyway, your mother would miss you as soon as they got home."

A frightened look in Becky's face brought Tom to his senses and he saw that he had made a blunder. Becky was not to have gone home that night! The children became silent and thoughtful. In a moment a new burst of grief from Becky showed Tom that the thing in his mind had struck hers also—that the Sabbath morning might be half spent before Mrs. Thatcher discovered that Becky was not at Mrs. Harper's.

The children fastened their eyes upon their bit of candle and watched it melt slowly and pitilessly away; saw the half-inch of wick stand alone at last; saw the feeble flame rise and fall, climb the thin column of smoke, linger at its top a moment, and then— the horror of utter darkness reigned!

How long afterward it was that Becky came to a slow consciousness that she was crying in Tom's arms, neither could tell. All that they knew was, that after what seemed a mighty stretch of time, both awoke out of a dead stupor of sleep and resumed their miseries once more. Tom said it might be Sunday, now—maybe Monday. He tried to get Becky to talk, but her sorrows were too oppressive, all her hopes were gone. Tom said they must have been missed long ago, and no doubt the search was going on. He would shout and maybe some one would come. He tried it; but in the darkness the distant echoes sounded so hideously that he tried it no more.

The hours wasted away, and hunger came to torment the captives again. A portion of Tom's half of the cake was left; they divided and ate it. But they seemed hungrier than before. The poor morsel of food only whetted desire.

By and by Tom said:

"'*Sh!* Did you hear that?"

Both held their breath and listened. There was a sound like the faintest, far-off shout. Instantly Tom answered it, and, leading Becky by the hand, started groping down the corridor in its direction. Presently he listened again; again the sound was heard, and apparently a little nearer.

"It's them!" said Tom; "they're coming! Come along, Becky— we're all right now!"

The joy of the prisoners was almost overwhelming. Their speed was slow, however, because pitfalls were somewhat common, and had to be guarded against. They shortly came to one and had to stop. It might be three feet deep, it might be a hundred—there was no passing it, at any rate. Tom got down on his breast and reached as far down as he could. No bottom. They must stay there and wait until the searchers came. They listened; evidently the distant shoutings were growing more distant! a moment or two more and they had gone altogether. The heart-sinking misery of it! Tom whooped until he was hoarse, but it was of no use. He talked hopefully to Becky; but an age of anxious waiting passed and no sounds came again.

The children groped their way back to the spring. The weary

time dragged on; they slept again, and awoke famished and woe-stricken. Tom believed it must be Tuesday by this time.

Now an idea struck him. There were some side passages near at hand. It would be better to explore some of these than bear the weight of the heavy time in idleness. He took a kiteline from his pocket, tied it to a projection, and he and Becky started, Tom in the lead, unwinding the line as he groped along. At the end of twenty steps the corridor ended in a "jumping-off place." Tom got down on his knees and felt below, and then as far around the corner as he could reach with his hands conveniently; he made an effort to stretch yet a little farther to the right, and at that moment, not twenty yards away, a human hand, holding a candle, appeared from behind a rock! Tom lifted up a glorious shout, and instantly that hand was followed by the body it belonged to—Injun Joe's! Tom was paralyzed; he could not move. He was vastly gratified the next moment to see the "Spaniard" take to his heels and get himself out of sight. Tom was careful to keep from Becky what it was he had seen. He told her he had only shouted "for luck."

But hunger and wretchedness rise superior to fears in the long run. Another tedious wait at the spring and another long sleep brought changes. The children awoke tortured with a raging hunger. Tom believed that it must be Wednesday or Thursday or even Friday or Saturday, now, and that the search had been given over. He proposed to explore another passage. He felt willing to risk Injun Joe and all other terrors. But Becky was very weak. She had sunk into a dreary apathy and would not be roused. She said she would wait, now, where she was, and die—it would not be long. She told Tom to go with the kite-line and explore if he chose; but she implored him to come back every little while and speak to her; and she made him promise that when the awful time came, he would stay by her and hold her hand until all was over.

Tom kissed her, with a choking sensation in his throat, and made a show of being confident of finding the searchers or an escape from the cave; then he took the kite-line in his hand and went groping down one of the passages on his hands and knees, distressed with hunger and sick with bodings of coming doom.

Tuesday afternoon came, and waned to the twilight. The village of St. Petersburg still mourned. The lost children had not been found. Public prayers had been offered up for them, and many and many a private prayer that had the petitioner's whole heart in it; but still no good news came from the cave. The majority of the searchers had given up the quest and gone back to their daily vocations, saying that it was plain the children could never be found. Mrs. Thatcher was very ill, and a great part of the time delirious. People said it was heartbreaking to hear her call her child, and raise her head and listen a whole minute at a time, then lay it wearily down again with a moan. Aunt Polly had drooped into a settled melancholy, and her gray hair had grown almost white. The village went to its rest on Tuesday night, sad and forlorn.

Away in the middle of the night a wild peal burst from the village bells, and in a moment the streets were swarming with frantic half-clad people, who shouted, "Turn out! turn out! they're found! they're found!" Tin pans and horns were added to the din, the population massed itself and moved toward the river, met the children coming in an open carriage drawn by shouting citizens, thronged around it, joined its homeward march, and swept magnificently up the main street roaring huzzah after huzzah!

The village was illuminated; nobody went to bed again; it was the greatest night the little town had ever seen. During the first half-hour a procession of villagers filed through Judge Thatcher's house, seized the saved ones and kissed them, squeezed Mrs. Thatcher's hand, tried to speak but couldn't—and drifted out raining tears all over the place.

Aunt Polly's happiness was complete, and Mrs. Thatcher's nearly so. It would be complete, however, as soon as the messenger dispatched with the great news to the cave should get the word to her husband. Tom lay upon a sofa with an eager auditory about him and told the history of the wonderful adventure, putting in many striking additions to adorn it withal; and closed with a description of how he left Becky and went on an exploring expedition; how he followed two avenues as far as his kite-line would reach; how he followed a third to the fullest stretch of the kite-line, and was about to turn back when he glimpsed a far-off speck that looked like daylight; dropped the line and groped toward it, pushed his head and shoulders through a small hole and saw the broad Mississippi rolling by! And if it had only happened to be night he would not have seen that speck of daylight and would not have explored that passage any more! He told how he went back for Becky and broke the good news and she told him not to fret her with such stuff, for she was tired, and knew she was going to die, and wanted to. He described how he labored with her and convinced her; and how she almost died for joy when she had groped to where she actually saw the blue speck of daylight; how he pushed his way out at the hole and then helped her out; how they sat there and cried for gladness; how some men came along in a skiff and Tom hailed them and told them their situation and their famished condition; how the men didn't believe the wild tale at first, "because," said they, "you are five miles down the river below the valley the cave is in"—then took them aboard, rowed to a house, gave them supper, made them rest till two or three hours after dark, and then brought them home.

Before day-dawn, Judge Thatcher and the handful of searchers with him were tracked out, in the cave, by the twine clews they had strung behind them, and informed of the great news.

Three days and nights of toil and hunger in the cave were not to be shaken off at once, as Tom and Becky soon discovered. They were bedridden all of Wednesday and Thursday, and seemed to grow more and more tired and worn all the time. Tom got about a little on Thursday, was downtown Friday, and nearly as whole as ever Saturday; but Becky did not leave her room until Sunday, and then she looked as if she had passed through a wasting illness.

Tom learned of Huck's sickness and went to see him on Friday, but could not be admitted to the bedroom; neither could he on Saturday or Sunday. He was admitted daily after that, but was warned to keep still about his adventure and introduce no exciting topic. The Widow Douglas stayed by to see that he obeyed. At home Tom learned of the Cardiff Hill event; also that the "ragged man's" body had eventually been found in the river near the ferry landing; he had been drowned while trying to escape, perhaps.

About a fortnight after Tom's rescue from the cave, he started off to visit Huck, who had grown plenty strong enough, now, to hear exciting talk, and Tom had some that would interest him, he thought. Judge Thatcher's house was on Tom's way, and he stopped to see Becky. The Judge and some friends set Tom to talking, and some one asked him ironically if he wouldn't like to go to the cave again. Tom said he thought he wouldn't mind it. The Judge said:

"Well, there are others just like you, Tom, I've not the least doubt. But we have taken care of that. Nobody will get lost in that cave any more."

"Why?"

"Because I had its big door sheathed with boiler iron two weeks ago, and triple-locked—and I've got the keys."

Tom turned as white as a sheet.

"What's the matter, boy! Here, run, somebody! Fetch a glass of water!"

The water was brought and thrown into Tom's face.

"Ah, now you're all right. What was the matter with you, Tom?"

"Oh, Judge, Injun Joe's in the cave!"

Within a few minutes the news had spread, and a dozen skiff-loads of men were on their way to McDougal's cave, and the ferry-boat, well filled with passengers, soon followed. Tom Sawyer was in the skiff that bore Judge Thatcher.

When the cave door was unlocked, a sorrowful sight presented itself in the dim twilight of the place. Injun Joe lay stretched upon the ground, dead, with his face close to the crack of the door, as if his longing eyes had been fixed, to the latest moment, upon the light and the cheer of the free world outside. Tom was touched, for he knew by his own experience how this wretch had suffered. His pity was moved, but nevertheless he felt an abounding sense of relief and security, now, which revealed to him in a degree which he had not fully appreciated before how a vast weight of dread had been lying upon him since the day he lifted his voice against this bloody-minded outcast.

Injun Joe's bowie-knife lay close by, its blade broken in two. The great foundation-beam of the door had been chipped and hacked through, with tedious labor; useless labor, too, it was, for the native rock formed a sill outside it, and upon that stubborn material the knife had wrought no effect; the only damage done was to the knife itself. But if there had been no stony obstruction there the labor would have been useless still, for if the beam had been wholly cut away Injun Joe could not have squeezed his body under the door, and he knew it. So he had only hacked that place in order to be doing something—in order to pass the weary time—in order to employ his tortured faculties. Ordinarily one could find half a dozen bits of candle stuck around in the crevices of this vestibule, left there by tourists; but there were none now. The prisoner had searched them out and eaten them. He had also contrived to catch a few bats, and these, also, he had eaten, leaving only their claws. The poor unfortunate had starved to death. In one place near at hand, a stalagmite had been slowly growing up from the ground for ages, builded by the water-drip from a stalactite overhead. The captive had broken off the stalagmite, and upon the stump had placed a stone, wherein he had scooped a shallow hollow to catch the precious drop that fell once in every three minutes with the dreary regularity of a clock-tick—a dessert-spoonful once in four-and-twenty hours.

Injun Joe was buried near the mouth of the cave; and people flocked there in boats and wagons from the towns and from all the farms and hamlets for seven miles around; they brought their children, and all sorts of provisions, and confessed that they had

had almost as satisfactory a time at the funeral as they could have had at the hanging.

This funeral stopped the further growth of one thing—the petition to the Governor for Injun Joe's pardon. The petition had been largely signed; many tearful and eloquent meetings had been held, and a committee of sappy women been appointed to go in deep mourning and wail around the Governor, and implore him to be a merciful ass and trample his duty under foot. Injun Joe was believed to have killed five citizens of the village, but what of that? If he had been Satan himself there would have been plenty of weaklings ready to scribble their names to a pardon petition, and drip a tear on it from their permanently impaired and leaky waterworks.

The morning after the funeral Tom took Huck to a private place to have an important talk. Huck had learned all about Tom's adventure from the Welshman and the Widow Douglas, by this time, but Tom said he reckoned there was one thing they had not told him; that thing was what he wanted to talk about now. Huck's face saddened. He said:

"I know what it is. You got into No. 2 and never found anything but whisky. Nobody told me it was you; but I just knowed it must 'a' ben you, soon as I heard 'bout that whisky business; and I knowed you hadn't got the money becuz you'd 'a' got at me some way or other and told me even if you was mum to everybody else. Tom, something's always told me we'd never get holt of that swag."

"Why, Huck, *I* never told on that tavern-keeper. *You* know his tavern was all right the Saturday I went to the picnic. Don't you remember you was to watch there that night?"

"Oh, yes! Why, it seems 'bout a year ago. It was that very night that I follered Injun Joe to the widder's."

"*You* followed him?"

"Yes—but you keep mum. I reckon Injun Joe's left friends behind him, and I don't want 'em souring on me and doing me mean tricks. If it hadn't been for me he'd be down in Texas now."

Then Huck told his entire adventure in confidence to Tom, who had only heard of the Welshmen's part of it before.

"Well," said Huck, presently, coming back to the main question, "whoever nipped the whisky in No. 2 nipped the money, too, I reckon—anyways it's a goner for us, Tom."

"Huck, that money wasn't ever in No. 2!"

"What!" Huck searched his comrade's face keenly. "Tom, have you got on the track of that money again?"

"Huck, it's in the cave!"

Huck's eyes blazed.

"Say it again, Tom."

"The money's in the cave!"

"Tom—honest injun, now—is it fun or earnest?"

"Earnest, Huck—just as earnest as ever I was in my life. Will you go in there with me and help get it out?"

"I bet I will! I will if it's where we can blaze our way to it and not get lost."

"Huck, we can do that without the least little bit of trouble in the world."

"Good as wheat! What makes you think the money's—"

"Huck, you just wait till we get in there. If we don't find it I'll agree to give you my drum and everything I've got in the world. I will, by jings."

"All right—it's a whiz. When do you say?"

"Right now, if you say it. Are you strong enough?"

"Is it far in the cave? I ben on my pins a little, three or four days, now, but I can't walk more'n a mile, Tom—least I don't think I could."

"It's about five mile into there the way anybody but me would go, Huck, but there's a mighty short cut that they don't anybody but me know about. Huck, I'll take you right to it in a skiff. I'll float the skiff down there, and I'll pull it back again all by myself. You needn't ever turn your hand over."

"Less start right off, Tom."

"All right. We want some bread and meat, and our pipes, and a little bag or two, and two or three kite-strings, and some of these new-fangled things they call lucifer matches. I tell you, many's the time I wished I had some when I was in there before."

A trifle after noon the boys borrowed a small skiff from a citizen who was absent, and got under way at once. When they were several miles below "Cave Hollow," Tom said:

"Now you see this bluff here looks all alike all the way down from the cave hollow—no houses, no woodyards, bushes all alike. But do you see that white place up yonder where there's been a landslide? Well, that's one of my marks. We'll get ashore, now."

They landed.

"Now, Huck, where we're a-standing you could touch that hole I got out of with a fishing-pole. See if you can find it."

Huck searched all the place about, and found nothing. Tom proudly marched into a thick clump of sumach bushes and said:

"Here you are! Look at it, Huck; it's the snuggest hole in this country. You just keep mum about it. All along I've been wanting to be a robber, but I knew I'd got to have a thing like this, and where to run across it was the bother. We've got it now, and we'll keep it quiet, only we'll let Joe Harper and Ben Rogers in— because of course there's got to be a Gang, or else there wouldn't be any style about it. Tom Sawyer's Gang—it sounds splendid, don't it, Huck?"

"Well, it just does, Tom. And who'll we rob?"

"Oh, most anybody. Waylay people—that's mostly the way."

"And kill them?"

"No, not always. Hide them in the cave till they raise a ransom."

"What's a ransom?"

"Money. You make them raise all they can, off'n their friends; and after you've kept them a year, if it ain't raised then you kill them. That's the general way. Only you don't kill the women. You shut up the women, but you don't kill them. They're always beautiful and rich, and awfully scared. You take their watches and things, but you always take your hat off and talk polite. They ain't anybody as polite as robbers—you'll see that in any book. Well, the women get to loving you, and after they've been in the cave a week or two weeks they stop crying and after that you couldn't get them to leave. If you drove them out they'd turn right around and come back. It's so in all the books."

"Why, it's real bully, Tom. I b'lieve it's better'n to be a pirate."

"Yes, it's better in some ways, because it's close to home and circuses and all that."

By this time everything was ready and the boys entered the hole, Tom in the lead. They toiled their way to the farther end of the tunnel, then made their spliced kite-strings fast and moved on. A few steps brought them to the spring, and Tom felt a shudder quiver all through him. He showed Huck the fragment of candle-wick perched on a lump of clay against the wall, and described how he and Becky had watched the flame struggle and expire.

The boys began to quiet down to whispers, now, for the stillness and gloom of the place oppressed their spirits. They went on, and presently entered and followed Tom's other corridor until they reached the "jumping-off place." The candles revealed the fact that it was not really a precipice, but only a steep clay hill twenty or thirty feet high. Tom whispered:

"Now I'll show you something, Huck."

He held his candle aloft and said:

"Look as far around the corner as you can. Do you see that? There—on the big rock over yonder—done with candle-smoke."

"Tom, it's a *cross!*"

"*Now* where's your Number Two? '*Under the cross,*' hey? Right yonder's where I saw Injun Joe poke up his candle, Huck!"

Huck stared at the mystic sign awhile, and then said with a shaky voice:

"Tom, le's git out of here!"

"What! and leave the treasure?"

"Yes—leave it. Injun Joe's ghost is round about there, certain."

"No it ain't, Huck, no it ain't. It would ha'nt the place where he died—away out at the mouth of the cave—five miles from here."

"No, Tom, it wouldn't. It would hang round the money. I know the ways of ghosts, and so do you."

Tom began to fear that Huck was right. Misgivings gathered in his mind. But presently an idea occurred to him—

"Looky here, Huck, what fools we're making of ourselves! Injun Joe's ghost ain't a-going to come around where there's a cross!"

The point was well taken. It had its effect.

"Tom, I didn't think of that. But that's so. It's luck for us, that cross is. I reckon we'll climb down there and have a hunt for that box."

Tom went first, cutting rude steps in the clay hill as he descended. Huck followed. Four avenues opened out of the small cavern which the great rock stood in. The boys examined three of them with no result. They found a small recess in the one nearest the base of the rock, with a pallet of blankets spread down in it; also an old suspender, some bacon rind, and the well-gnawed bones of two or three fowls. But there was no money-box. The lads searched and re-searched this place, but in vain. Tom said:

"He said *under* the cross. Well, this comes nearest to being under the cross. It can't be under the rock itself, because that sets solid on the ground."

They searched everywhere once more, and then sat down discouraged. Huck could suggest nothing. By and by Tom said:

"Looky here, Huck, there's footprints and some candle-grease on the clay about one side of this rock, but not on the other sides. Now, what's that for? I bet you the money *is* under the rock. I'm going to dig in the clay."

"That ain't no bad notion, Tom!" said Huck with animation.

Tom's "real Barlow" was out at once, and he had not dug four inches before he struck wood.

"Hey, Huck!—you hear that?"

Huck began to dig and scratch now. Some boards were soon uncovered and removed. They had concealed a natural chasm which led under the rock. Tom got into this and held his candle as far under the rock as he could, but said he could not see to the end of the rift. He proposed to explore. He stooped and passed under; the narrow way descended gradually. He followed its winding course, first to the right, then to the left, Huck at his heels. Tom turned a short curve, by and by, and exclaimed:

"My goodness, Huck, looky here!"

It was the treasure-box, sure enough, occupying a snug little cavern, along with an empty powder-keg, a couple of guns in leather cases, two or three pairs of old moccasins, a leather belt, and some other rubbish well soaked with the water-drip.

"Got it at last!" said Huck, plowing among the tarnished coins with his hand. "My, but we're rich, Tom!"

"Huck, I always reckoned we'd get it. It's just too good to believe, but we *have* got it, sure! Say—let's not fool around here. Let's snake it out. Lemme see if I can lift the box."

It weighed about fifty pounds. Tom could lift it, after an awkward fashion, but could not carry it conveniently.

"I thought so," he said; "*they* carried it like it was heavy, that day at the ha'nted house. I noticed that. I reckon I was right to think of fetching the little bags along."

The money was soon in the bags and the boys took it up to the cross rock.

"Now le's fetch the guns and things," said Huck.

"No, Huck—leave them there. They're just the tricks to have when we go to robbing. We'll keep them there all the time, and we'll hold our orgies there, too. It's an awful snug place for orgies."

"What's orgies?"

"*I* dono. But robbers always have orgies, and of course we've got to have them, too. Come along, Huck; we've been in here a long time. It's getting late, I reckon. I'm hungry, too. We'll eat and smoke when we get to the skiff."

They presently emerged into the clump of sumach bushes, looked warily out, found the coast clear, and were soon lunching and smoking in the skiff. As the sun dipped toward the horizon they pushed out and got under way. Tom skimmed up the shore through the long twilight, chatting cheerily with Huck, and landed shortly after dark.

"Now, Huck," said Tom, "we'll hide the money in the loft of the widow's woodshed, and I'll come up in the morning and we'll count it and divide, and then we'll hunt up a place out in the woods for it where it will be safe. Just you lay quiet here and watch the stuff till I run and hook Benny Taylor's little wagon; I won't be gone a minute."

He disappeared, and presently returned with the wagon, put the two small sacks into it, threw some old rags on top of them, and started off, dragging his cargo behind him. When the boys reached the Welshman's house, they stopped to rest. Just as they were about to move on, the Welshman stepped out and said:

"Hello, who's that?"

"Huck and Tom Sawyer."

"Good! Come along with me, boys; you are keeping everybody waiting. Here—hurry up, trot ahead—I'll haul the wagon for you. Why, it's not as light as it might be. Got bricks in it?—or old metal?"

"Old metal," said Tom.

"I judged so; the boys in this town will take more trouble and fool away more time hunting up six bits' worth of old iron to sell to the foundry than they would to make twice the money at regular work. But that's human nature—hurry along, hurry along!"

The boys wanted to know what the hurry was about.

"Never mind; you'll see when we get to the Widow Douglas's."

Huck said with some apprehension—for he was long used to being falsely accused:

"Mr. Jones, *we* haven't been doing nothing."

The Welshman laughed.

"Well, I don't know, Huck, my boy. I don't know about that. Ain't you and the widow good friends?"

"Yes. Well, she's ben good friends to me, anyways."

"All right, then. What do you want to be afraid for?"

This question was not entirely answered in Huck's slow mind before he found himself pushed, along with Tom, into Mrs. Douglas's drawing-room. Mr. Jones left the wagon near the door and followed.

The place was grandly lighted, and everybody that was of any consequence in the village was there. The Thatchers were there, the Harpers, the Rogerses, Aunt Polly, Sid, Mary, the minister, the editor, and a great many more and all dressed in their best. The widow received the boys as heartily as any one could well receive two such looking beings. They were covered with clay and candle-grease. Aunt Polly blushed crimson with humiliation, and frowned and shook her head at Tom. Nobody suffered half as much as the two boys did, however, Mr. Jones said:

"Tom wasn't at home, yet, so I gave him up; but I stumbled on him and Huck right at my door, and so I just brought them along in a hurry."

"And you did just right," said the widow. "Come with me, boys."

She took them to a bedchamber and said:

"Now wash and dress yourselves. Here are two new suits of clothes—shirts, socks, everything complete. They're Huck's—no, no thanks, Huck—Mr. Jones bought one and I the other. But they'll fit both of you. Get into them. We'll wait—come down when you are slicked up enough."

Then she left.

Huck said: "Tom, we can slope, if we can find a rope. The window ain't high from the ground."

"Shucks, what do you want to slope for?"

"Well, I ain't used to that kind of a crowd. I can't stand it. I ain't going down there, Tom."

"Oh, bother! It ain't anything. I don't mind it a bit. I'll take care of you."

Sid appeared.

"Tom," said he, "auntie has been waiting for you all the afternoon. Mary got your Sunday clothes ready, and everybody's been fretting about you. Say—ain't this grease and clay, on your clothes?"

"Now, Mr. Siddy, you jist 'tend to your own business. What's all this blow-out about, anyway?"

"It's one of the widow's parties that she's always having. This time it's for the Welshman and his sons, on account of that scrape they helped her out of the other night. And say—I can tell you something, if you want to know."

"Well, what?"

"Why, old Mr. Jones is going to try to spring something on the people here to-night, but I overheard him tell auntie to-day about it, as a secret, but I reckon it's not much of a secret *now*. Everybody knows—the widow, too, for all she tries to let on she don't. Mr. Jones was bound Huck should be here—couldn't get along with his grand secret without Huck, you know!"

"Secret about what, Sid?"

"About Huck tracking the robbers to the widow's. I reckon Mr. Jones was going to make a grand time over his surprise, but I bet you it will drop pretty flat."

Sid chuckled in a very contented and satisfied way.

"Sid, was it you that told?"

"Oh, never mind who it was. *Somebody* told—that's enough."

"Sid, there's only one person in this town mean enough to do that, and that's you. If you had been in Huck's place you'd 'a' sneaked down the hill and never told anybody on the robbers. You can't do any but mean things, and you can't bear to see anybody praised for doing good ones. There—no thanks, as the widow says"—and Tom cuffed Sid's ears and helped him to the door with several kicks. "Now go and tell auntie if you dare—and tomorrow you'll catch it!"

Some minutes later the widow's guests were at the supper-table, and a dozen children were propped up at little side-tables in the same room, after the fashion of that country and that day. At the proper time Mr. Jones made his little speech, in which he thanked the widow for the honor she was doing himself and his sons, but said that there was another person whose modesty—

And so forth and so on. He sprung his secret about Huck's share in the adventure in the finest dramatic manner he was master of, but the surprise it occasioned was largely counterfeit and not as clamorous and effusive as it might have been under happier circumstances. However, the widow made a pretty fair show of astonishment, and heaped so many compliments and so much gratitude upon Huck that he almost forgot the nearly intolerable discomfort of his new clothes in the entirely intolerable discomfort of being set up as a target for everybody's gaze and everybody's laudations.

The widow said she meant to give Huck a home under her roof and have him educated; and that when she could spare the money she would start him in business in a modest way. Tom's chance was come. He said:

"Huck don't need it. Huck's rich."

Nothing but a heavy strain upon the good manners of the company kept back the due and proper complimentary laugh at this pleasant joke. But the silence was a little awkward. Tom broke it:

"Huck's got money. Maybe you don't believe it, but he's got lots of it. Oh, you needn't smile—I reckon I can show you. You just wait a minute."

Tom ran out of doors. The company looked at each other with a perplexed interest—and inquiringly at Huck, who was tongue-tied.

"Sid, what ails Tom?" said Aunt Polly. "He—well, there ain't ever any making of that boy out. I never—"

Tom entered, struggling with the weight of his sacks, and Aunt Polly did not finish her sentence. Tom poured the mass of yellow coin upon the table and said:

"There—what did I tell you? Half of it's Huck's and half of it's mine!"

The spectacle took the general breath away. All gazed, nobody spoke for a moment. Then there was a unanimous call for an explanation. Tom said he could furnish it, and he did. The tale was long, but brimful of interest. There was scarcely an interruption from any one to break the charm of its flow. When he had finished, Mr. Jones said:

"I thought I had fixed up a little surprise for this occasion, but it don't amount to anything now. This one makes it sing mighty small, I'm willing to allow."

The money was counted. The sum amounted to a little over twelve thousand dollars. It was more than any one present had ever seen at one time before, though several persons were there who were worth considerably more than that in property.

The reader may rest satisfied that Tom's and Huck's windfall made a mighty stir in the poor little village of St. Petersburg. So vast a sum, all in actual cash, seemed next to incredible. It was talked about, gloated over, glorified, until the reason of many of the citizens tottered under the strain of the unhealthy excitement. Every "haunted" house in St. Petersburg and the neighboring villages was dissected, plank by plank, and its foundations dug up and ransacked for hidden treasure—and not by boys, but men— pretty grave, unromantic men, too, some of them. Wherever Tom and Huck appeared they were courted, admired, stared at. The boys were not able to remember that their remarks had possessed weight before; but now their sayings were treasured and repeated; everything they did seemed somehow to be regarded as remarkable; they had evidently lost the power of doing and saying commonplace things; moreover, their past history was raked up and discovered to bear marks of conspicuous originality. The village paper published biographical sketches of the boys.

The Widow Douglas put Huck's money out at six per cent, and Judge Thatcher did the same with Tom's at Aunt Polly's request. Each lad had an income, now, that was simply prodigious—a dollar for every week-day in the year and half of the Sundays. It was just what the minister got—no, it was what he was promised —he generally couldn't collect it. A dollar and a quarter a week would board, lodge, and school a boy in those simple days—and clothe him and wash him, too, for that matter.

Judge Thatcher had conceived a great opinion of Tom. He said that no commonplace boy would ever have got his daughter out of the cave. When Becky told her father, in strict confidence, how

Tom had taken her whipping at school, the Judge was visibly moved; and when she pleaded grace for the mighty lie Tom had told in order to shift that whipping from her shoulders to his own, the Judge said with a fine outburst that it was noble, a generous, a magnanimous lie—a lie that was worthy to hold up its head and march down through history breast to breast with George Washington's lauded Truth about the hatchet! Becky thought her father had never looked so tall and so superb as when he walked the floor and stamped his foot and said that. She went straight off and told Tom about it.

Judge Thatcher hoped to see Tom a great lawyer or a great soldier some day. He said he meant to look to it that Tom should be admitted to the National Military Academy and afterward trained in the best law school in the country, in order that he might be ready for either career or both.

Huck Finn's wealth and the fact that he was now under the Widow Douglas's protection introduced him into society—no, dragged him into it, hurled him into it—and his sufferings were almost more than he could bear. The widow's servants kept him clean and neat, combed and brushed, and they bedded him nightly in unsympathetic sheets that had not one little spot or stain which he could press to his heart and know for a friend. He had to eat with knife and fork; he had to use napkin, cup, and plate; he had to learn his book, he had to go to church; he had to talk so properly that speech was become insipid in his mouth; withersoever he turned, the bars and shackles of civilization shut him in and bound him hand and foot.

He bravely bore his miseries three weeks, and then one day turned up missing. For forty-eight hours the widow hunted for him everywhere in great distress. The public were profoundly concerned; they searched high and low, they dragged the river for his body. Early the third morning Tom Sawyer wisely went poking among some old empty hogsheads down behind the abandoned slaughter-house, and in one of them he found the refugee. Huck had slept there; he had just breakfasted upon some stolen odds and ends of food, and was lying off, now, in comfort, with his pipe. He was unkempt, uncombed, and clad in the same old ruin of rags that had made him picturesque in the days when he was free and happy. Tom routed him out, told him the trouble he had been causing, and urged him to go home. Huck's face lost its tranquil content, and took a melancholy cast. He said:

"Don't talk about it, Tom. I've tried it, and it don't work; it don't work, Tom. It ain't for me; I ain't used to it. The widder's good to me, and friendly; but I can't stand them ways. She makes me git up just the same time every morning; she makes me wash, they comb me all to thunder; she won't let me sleep in the woodshed; I got to wear them blamed clothes that just smothers me, Tom; they don't seem to let any air git through 'em, somehow; and they're so rotten nice that I can't set down, nor lay down, nor roll around anywher's; I hain't slid on a cellar-door for —well, it 'pears to be years; I got to go to church and sweat and sweat—I hate them ornery sermons! I can't ketch a fly in there, I can't chaw. I got to wear shoes all Sunday. The widder eats by a bell; she goes to bed by a bell; she gits up by a bell—everything's so awful reg'lar a body can't stand it."

"Well, everybody does that way, Huck."

"Tom, it don't make no difference. I ain't everybody, and I can't *stand* it. It's awful to be tied up so. And grub comes too easy —I don't take no interest in vittles, that way. I got to ask to go a-fishing; I got to ask to go in a-swimming—dern'd if I hain't got to ask to do everything. Well, I'd got to talk so nice it wasn't no comfort—I'd got to go up in the attic and rip out awhile, every day, to git a taste in my mouth, or I'd 'a' died, Tom. The widder wouldn't let me smoke; she wouldn't let me yell, she wouldn't let me gape, nor stretch, nor scratch, before folks——" [Then with a spasm of special irritation and injury]—"And dad fetch it, she prayed all the time! I never *see* such a woman! I *had* to shove, Tom —I just had to. And besides, that school's going to open, and I'd 'a' had to go to it—well, I wouldn't stand *that*, Tom. Looky here, Tom, being rich ain't what it's cracked up to be. It's just worry and worry, and sweat and sweat, and a-wishing you was dead all the time. Now these clothes suits me, and this bar'l suits me, and I ain't ever going to shake 'em any more. Tom, I wouldn't ever got into all this trouble if it hadn't 'a' been for that money; now you just take my sheer of it along with your'n, and gimme a ten-center sometimes—not many times, becuz I don't give a dern for a thing 'thout it's tollable hard to git—and you go and beg off for me with the widder."

"Oh, Huck, you know I can't do that. 'Tain't fair; and, besides, if you'll try this thing just awhile longer you'll come to like it."

"Like it! Yes—the way I'd like a hot stove if I was to set on it long enough. No, Tom, I won't be rich, and I won't live in them cussed smothery houses. I like the woods, and the river, and hogsheads, and I'll stick to 'em, too. Blame it all! just as we'd got guns, and a cave, and all just fixed to rob, here this dern foolishness has got to come up and spile it all!"

Tom saw his opportunity——

"Looky here, Huck, being rich ain't going to keep me back from turning robber."

"No! Oh, good-licks, are you in real deadwood earnest, Tom?"

"Just as dead earnest as I'm a-sitting here. But, Huck, we can't let you into the gang if you ain't respectable, you know."

Huck's joy was quenched.

"Can't let me in, Tom? Didn't you let me go for a pirate?"

"Yes, but that's different. A robber is more high-toned than what a pirate is—as a general thing. In most countries they're awful high up in the nobility—dukes and such."

"Now, Tom, hain't you always ben friendly to me? You wouldn't shet me out, would you, Tom? You wouldn't do that, now, *would* you, Tom?"

"Huck, I wouldn't want to, and I *don't* want to—but what would people say? Why, they'd say, 'Mph! Tom Sawyer's Gang! pretty low characters in it!' They'd mean you, Huck. You wouldn't like that, and I wouldn't."

Huck was silent for some time, engaged in a mental struggle.

Finally he said:

"Well, I'll go back to the widder for a month and tackle it and see if I can come to stand it, if you'll let me b'long to the gang, Tom."

"All right, Huck, it's a whiz! Come along, old chap, and I'll ask the widow to let up on you a little, Huck."

"Will you, Tom—now will you? That's good. If she'll let up on some of the roughest things, I'll smoke private and cuss private, and crowd through or bust. When you going to start the gang and turn robbers?"

"Oh, right off. We'll get the boys together and have the initiation to-night, maybe."

"Have the which?"

"Have the initiation."

"What's that?"

"It's to swear to stand by one another, and never tell the gang's secrets, even if you're chopped all to flinders, and kill anybody and all his family that hurts one of the gang."

"That' gay—that's mighty gay, Tom, I tell you."

"Well, I bet it is. And all that swearing's got to be done at midnight, in the lonesomest, awfulest place you can find—a ha'nted house is the best, but they're all ripped up now."

"Well, midnight's good, anyway, Tom."

"Yes, so it is. And you've got to swear on a coffin, and sign it with blood."

"Now, that's something *like!* Why, it's a million times bullier than pirating. I'll stick to the widder till I rot, Tom; and if I git to be a reg'lar ripper of a robber, and everybody talking 'bout it, I reckon she'll be proud she snaked me in out of the wet."

THE MYSTERY IN
FOUR-AND-A-HALF STREET

DONALD AND LOUISE PEATTIE

"You can't keep me here after tomorrow," Chuck Ames told the great ugly grandfather clock in the corner of the musty curiosity shop. "I'm quitting. I'm no antique clerk!"

It was a relief to say something aloud, even if you only growled it at the old clock. Sitting there on a high stool behind the cluttered counter, with an hour or more between customers, was the deadest job on earth.

"And I thought I was pretty good to land it," Chuck reflected. "Pretty good! Well, that was over a week ago, and I was a lot younger. I know better now."

Chuck wouldn't have admitted it but he was talking to keep up his courage. He felt somehow unreasonably wary—on guard. Was there something queer about the dreary little shop and fat Utterback, its owner? Or was he just imagining it? Probably the latter. But it was uncomfortable to feel so wary.

Anyhow, he was getting out. But that was depressing too. He had been so glad to get in.

It had been on the day after Chuck had been graduated from high school that he had found Utterback's advertisement in the *News*.

> WANTED: *Bright, reliable, discreet boy as*
> *clerk in curiosity shop. Good wages. Apply*
> *13 Four-and-a-Half Street.*

Chuck had applied immediately, he had landed the job, and the wages *were* good. It had been on the strength of those wages that he had packed off his mother, with whom he lived alone, down to the seashore for the first rest she had had in ten years.

For three days he had hopefully tried to sell some of the junk that filled the ramshackle narrow building on Four-and-a-Half Street, which was a slantwise alley one block long, almost lost in a dingy quarter of the city. At the end of those three days he had waylaid his employer, a man with fat white flesh like lard and eyes like blue "mibs" set under colorless eyebrows.

"I'm sorry to inconvenience you, Mr. Utterback," Chuck had said, a little flushed, "but I'll be leaving you at the end of a week. I don't believe I'll ever be much good at work like this."

The fat man had given him an opaque glance, grunted assent, tilted his derby farther over his lashless eyes, and lumbered on out.

Utterback spent little time in the shop. Occasionally he was there to meet some special customers, and these men he led up to his living quarters on the third floor—the second was filled with second-hand furniture—and there transacted business.

What that business was Chuck had had plenty of time to wonder. He had had time enough to develop a puzzled distrust of the trade that went on under the dingy sign, *Antique Shoppe,* hung over the door of Number 13. Few customers came in for any of the tawdry wares of the shop—rococo lamps, plaster statuary, oil paintings of dead mallard ducks, goldfish castles, atrocious imitations of Chinese vases, shaky tables, crack-bottomed chairs, and cheap jewelry. The show window made some pretense of living up to the sign above it, holding a few candlesticks, some snuffboxes, and a tray of old semi-precious jewels of which the chief boast was a flawed square-cut emerald.

That tray, Utterback had impressed upon Chuck, was to be his responsibility. He was to keep his eye on it when strangers were in the shop, and at night he was to put it into the desk drawer, lock that, and leave the key on the safe at the back of the shop. Sitting through the dull hours behind the cluttered counter, Chuck had rumpled his thick brown hair and wondered why Utterback didn't keep the tray of jewels in the safe. What else was the safe for?

To Chuck, the whole air of Number 13 was furtive. The dingiest of its secrets was brought to light when a shabby woman or a ragged man came slipping into the shop with something wrapped in crumpled paper or hidden under a worn coat. When Utterback was there he turned the offered object over in his fat hands, sneeringly, and named a loan of a few cents in a contemptuous grunt. When Chuck was alone, he gave a receipt for the proffered security, and told the customer to come back later to settle with the pawnbroker.

"It's a mean business," Chuck growled, sitting there frowning on top of his high stool. "I'd rather dig ditches."

Well, tomorrow was the last day. One hour till closing time tonight. He spent that hour watching the slow-moving hand on the face of the old grandfather clock. The clock had come to seem a jailer to him, a big stout ugly jailer breathing with a ponderous ticking.

At last it boomed six slow strokes. Utterback came lumbering down the stairs, let Chuck out the front door, and locked it after him. The boy stood in the dusty heat of Four-and-a-Half Street, and heaved a sigh of relief.

The gray-haired blind man who sold pencils on the opposite corner had shut up his box and was slowly, cautiously, starting for home. At the curb he paused, listening, his stick clutched anxiously. Chuck darted forward and took the man's arm.

"Thank you, boy." The blind man's quick smile was pleasant, almost youthful, and his voice was silvery, like his hair.

"How did you know I was a boy?" asked Chuck, guiding across the street.

"When this sense is gone—" the peddler tapped the black glasses—"this one gets sharper." He touched his ear. "A boy's lively, light step—it's as easy to read as a face. Well, here my way turns. Thank you for your thoughtfulness."

And he went on up the drab street, the tap-tap of his cane vanishing in the city noises.

Chuck got his dinner at a little restaurant and then, feeling lonely in the summer evening, dropped into a movie theater that was showing a promising Western. Carried away by the sweep of the desert and the gallop of hoofs, he was forgetting his mean job, and the problem of getting a better one, when a sudden recollection came upon him.

He hadn't put that window tray of trinkets into the desk drawer!

He ought to go back and do it, he thought reluctantly. Yet Mr. Utterback might take care of the tray, and anyway it would probably be safe enough. Chuck sat still. On the screen the sheriff's posse was galloping to the relief of the heroine locked in the blazing telegraph office. But at last a persistent prick of his conscience got Chuck out of his comfortable seat, and with a sigh he tramped back to the shop.

The summer dark was close and stuffy in Four-and-a-Half Street. The buildings down the block were lightless; they loomed up blackly—two warehouses, an old office building condemned as a fire trap, the greasy Greek fruit store, shut for the night, and Utterback's "Antique Shoppe." At the end of the block a single violet arc light sputtered. Distantly, Chuck could hear the clamor of street cars and the rush of traffic, but the slantwise strip of street seemed a sinister island of silence in the life of the city.

He could just make out the tray of jewels safe in the shop front. Scowling at it, he told himself he had been a fool to bother to come back. Still, here he was and if the pawnbroker were in, he might as well confess he had forgotten to put away the jewels. He rang the doorbell and waited, staring in the dim shop window.

The bell sent faint echoes through the rambling old house; beyond the dusty glass, shadows seemed to waver in the dark shop.

"This place gets creepier than ever at night," Chuck muttered. He had to persuade himself out of the notion that eyes were watching him from the black doorway of the warehouse opposite. Better go home and forget the silly business; no one answered the bell.

But there was a stubborn streak in Chuck. And after all, putting away that tray with its probably valuable emerald was part of his job.

He'd go around to the back, he decided, and call up to Utterback's window, on the chance he was in and hadn't heard the bell.

The light in the alley was faint, a dim blue wash. The third floor was dark—was Utterback out, or asleep? Chuck cupped his hands round his mouth for a shout, and then his eyes fell to the shop's back door, and he choked back his shout to a gasp. The door was open!

He stepped closer. The staples of an obsolete outside padlock fastening remained, but the raw, splintered wood of the door frame told how the inside lock had yielded to an expert jimmy.

Only five minutes before, Chuck had seen the jewels untouched in the shop window. Then the thief, he reasoned swiftly, was now in the shop—perhaps at this moment laying hands on the square-cut emerald. He stood a moment listening and heard a faint sound like a stumble within.

There was no time to fume at himself for his carelessness. More than ever, the responsibility for that tray of trinkets lay on his head. Police in this quarter were few and far between. Without hesitation Chuck slipped noiselessly into the shop and flattened himself against the wall behind the door.

Somewhere in that thick darkness, where the big clock tick-tocked in hollow monotone, stood the burglar, doubtless startled to cautious waiting by Chuck's peal of the bell.

Unarmed, as he was, Chuck knew he had no chance with the burglar in an open fight. That was why he had swiftly decided to wait there in the shadow by the door until the burglar should start to leave and then leap on him from behind and get a grip on his windpipe. A desperate scheme, but the best he could fix on at the moment.

He waited, trying to smother the sound of his uneven breathing, listening to the grim tick-tock of the clock, staring with baffled eyes into the murky room lit only by the faint light of the arc lamp down the street, filtering in through the dirty glass of the shop front. Then the faintest scraping sound in the alley caught his attention, and he turned, holding his breath, to see through the crack of the open door the sudden blue spurt of a match flame.

The flickering little light illuminated the fingers that held it, thin, steely fingers. The next instant, through the crack, were visible too the silvery temples and black glasses of the blind pencil vendor, bent toward the jimmied door. The match went out. But as the implication of that brief, searching little flame struck home to Chuck, his skin crawled. The next thing he realized was that the door was closing, closing, slowly—and in a second he heard the muffled rattle and click of a padlock slipped through the staples and snapped into lock.

Through the thudding of his heart Chuck heard down the alley the stealthy footsteps of the blind man departing—the blind man who lighted matches in the dark.

A board creaked. Chuck's mind snapped back to the imperative fact that he was locked in the deserted shop with an unknown housebreaker. He had no idea why the door had been furtively padlocked on them. He had no idea where the thief was, or what his own next move should be. Why didn't his fellow prisoner make a sound—a move? Suddenly the answer to that hit Chuck like a blow. Sinkingly, he realized that that brief blue flame outside the door must have betrayed his presence, have shown his staring face in silhouette against the lighted door crack.

Yet, helpless, he still waited tensely in his corner. The silence was stifling. And out of that unbroken silence crept slowly to Chuck Ames a significance sharper than any outcry. The clock had stopped ticking.

In a flash he guessed why. That big clock case, with its long hinged door in front, held room for a burly six-footer, if he crouched. In his mind's eye Chuck could see the key in the clock door—he sent up an agonized prayer that it was in truth in the lock—and then slowly, soundlessly, he began to steal toward the clock. Six paces from it he caught the dim glint of the key in the

lock—his eyes were now accustomed to the darkness—and then beneath his foot a board treacherously cried out in the stillness.

He stood there, holding his breath and as he stood he saw the clock door slowly open and two fingers slide round the edge of it!

Lunging, he flung himself on the door. There was a strangled animal cry from within the case, the fingers jerked and vanished, and Chuck banged the door tight and turned the key in the lock. He heard the pounding of a shoulder on the stout oak door of the case as he ran to the wall switch and flooded the room with light.

Blinking, he stared at the tray of trinkets untouched in the window. He turned, and saw lying beside the safe at the back of the store a dark lantern, a chisel, a crowbar, and other tools less familiar. In another moment he was at the front door. It was locked, and the key gone.

Perhaps Utterback was in, after all—perhaps he had gone to bed, taking the key. It was a desperate hope, but Chuck dashed into the back hall, took the two flights three steps at a time, past the cluttered second floor ghostly with piles of old furniture, up to the floor of the pawnbroker's bedroom, whence issued a steady snoring. It was music to Chuck's ears. He pounded on the door.

"Mr. Utterback! Get up! Burglars!"

"Huh?" a thick sleepy voice grunted, and in a moment or two more a light flashed on in the room and the door opened on the pawnbroker's flabby figure, in a nightshirt hastily tucked into trousers.

"They were trying to break into the safe! I've locked the fellow in the clock!" panted Chuck.

Utterback's sleepiness vanished. "Into the safe!" Then his milky blue eyes narrowed to a dangerous slit. "What you doin' here at this time o' night, anyway? How'd you get in?"

Chuck started to explain but Utterback didn't wait to hear it all. He stepped back into the room for a moment, and reappeared with the deadly blue-black gleam of a revolver in his hand.

"Good!" cried Chuck. "That'll keep him in the clock till the police get here. Give me the key to the front door, sir, and I'll slip out and call Headquarters from the first phone I can get to."

"Get this," said Utterback, and there was sudden cold menace in his voice. "The police ain't in this—see? And anything you seen or will see around here tonight you're goin' to forget the minute you see it—see? Or you won't live to see daylight, kid—that's fair warning. Now get on with you."

With the cold muzzle of the gun sending chills up his spine Chuck turned and started down the black stairway, moving as in a nightmare.

This wasn't true. It was a dream. He had often dreamed it before. Dreamed of being forced down a stairway in a strange house, a stairway that wound down into blackness. Before him lay always unknown horrors; behind him, with heavy tread, something moved relentlessly upon him, driving him on and down. At the front of the stairs he always woke up, in a cold sweat of horror.

But now he was at the foot of the stairs, and light fell silently into the hall from the open door of the shop.

"Go on," said Utterback grimly, prodding him, and with Chuck a shield for the other's cowardly bulk, stepped into the room.

It was as before—the key still stood in the clock door.

"So there you are, Spike Brent!" Utterback addressed the invisible prisoner, with a malignant humor. "I see your favorite jimmy over there by the safe. Gettin' impatient, were you? Well, you can cool off in there till I get the stuff stowed away more secure, and then I'll see what to do with you."

No sound from the clock answered him. Utterback strode to the safe and with a few swift twists of the combination had the door open and, reaching in, drew out a little black felt bag. Except for some papers, there was nothing else in the big box of a safe. Utterback turned on the boy and motioned with his revolver.

"Get in," he said.

Chuck stared at him in horror, and stood frozen.

"Oh, I'll let you out before you're smothered," the fat man said, with an unpleasant laugh that showed pink gums. "But I want you out o' the way for a while—I'll be busy. Get in," he repeated less pleasantly.

"I won't!" Chuck jerked out.

Utterback's pink face changed to a menacing purple. "You young fool!" he growled. "You'll . . ."

At that second came the crash of a report—a shot muffled slightly by the thick oak door of the clock case, and out of the case leaped a big burly figure that hurled itself full upon Utterback!

The burglar had shot out the lock. Chuck's mind registered that fact mechanically, as he leaped out of the onslaught and stood pressed against the wall, while the two men struggled, swaying, panting, cursing.

Utterback held the black bag high out of reach. With a sudden plunge the burglar caught the fat wrist. He bent and twisted it till the pawnbroker with a scream of pain relaxed his hold on the prize and the bag, half flung from his hand, fell with a thud six paces away. Chuck Ames dived for the light switch and plunged the room in darkness. The next moment he had his hand on the bag, had caught it up, and was running noiselessly for the stairs.

Halfway up the first nightmare steps, however, he stumbled and fell with a clatter. He was up in a minute, but running feet pounded below, and just as he made the first landing the light hanging directly over his head went on, revealing him in its sudden glare plain as a target. With one leap and a swing of the heavy little bag, Chuck crashed out the light, and leaped on up into darkness.

On the dim second floor Chuck halted, panting. Clearly, through the turmoil of his mind, stood out the recollection of a gutter pipe running along the back door of the shop. If he could find a window near enough to it . . .

This floor was thrown into one loft where the furniture loomed in piles like great distorted monsters. Taking swift bearings, Chuck slipped through this confusion toward the corner where the gutter pipe ran. Feet were pounding up the stairs. If there were only a window . . .

There was. But it was locked, and he couldn't budge it. The feet had halted uncertainly on the threshold. All at once, cruel and garish, the light of a bulb flashed on in the ceiling—and the next moment Chuck had crashed the black bag through the pane, smashed out the glass, and swung over the sill.

A shot seared past him as he caught the gutter pipe and swung out on it. As he hit the ground in a supple jump, another shot rang out and pain caught him agonizingly by the shoulder. Dazed with agony but triumphant, Chuck doubled up and ran down the alley—straight into the staring muzzle of a revolver.

"Hands up!" said a familiar silvery voice, and Chuck with one sick look of horror at the black glasses of the "blind" man, crumpled with a groan into his own blood on the cobbles.

He opened his eyes upon cool dazzling whiteness. A hospital, he drowsily concluded, and shut them again. He heard the rustle of a starched uniform, and heard a woman's low voice say:

"He's coming to. You may speak to him if you want to."

And then he heard that odd, light, silvery man's voice again, that last voice out of his nightmare adventure.

"Good work, boy," it said. "Very neat. How are you feeling now?"

Chuck lifted his heavy lids, and warm brown eyes twinkled into his.

"Who are you?" gasped Chuck weakly.

"Tolliver's my name. Christopher C. Tolliver, investigator. I'm sorry—I had you doped out wrong, youngster. All wrong. I thought you were a spy for that gang down on Four-and-a-Half Street."

"I had you doped out wrong, too," said Chuck, blinking.

"I don't wonder," laughed the man. "Nobody on Four-and-a-Half Street is what he seems to be. Utterback looked like a pawn-broker and was really a fence for a gang of jewel thieves. What looked like a common burglar turns out to be Spike Brent, whom we've been wanting for two years. Spike got rash because Utterback was double-crossing him, and made a play to get back the famous Bramwell jewels he stole six years ago. And a kid who looked suspiciously like a cat's-paw turns out to be a darn valuable fellow with wit and nerve enough to balk two of the smartest crooks in the gallery. When you're patched up, we'll talk about a job I've got for you. Now slip off to sleep for a bit—you've lost a lot of blood."

And Chuck Ames, drowsily reflecting that the end of the Western couldn't have been half so thrilling as his evening had turned out to be, dozed off with a sleepy grin.